Y0-CLZ-159

37653001727497
Fletcher
MYSTERY ANDERSON
Death on the rocks

MYSTERY

**CENTRAL ARKANSAS LIBRARY SYSTEM
JOHN GOULD FLETCHER
BRANCH LIBRARY
LITTLE ROCK, ARKANSAS**

DEATH ON THE ROCKS

DEATH ON THE ROCKS

A NOVEL

by

J. R. L. ANDERSON

STEIN AND DAY/*Publishers*/New York

Author's Note

As the two maps show, the geographical setting of this story is real, and the Salcombe yawl, thank goodness, is a splendidly real boat. The human characters in the tale, however, are all imaginary, and bear no relationship to any real person.

First published in the United States of America in 1975
Copyright © 1973 by J. R. L. Anderson
All rights reserved
Printed in the United States of America
Stein and Day/*Publishers*/Scarborough House,
Briarcliff Manor, N.Y. 10510

Library of Congress Cataloging in Publication Data

Anderson, John Richard Lane, 1911—
Death on the rocks.
I. Title.
PZ4.A54755De3   (PR6051.N3934)   823'.9'14   74-26614
ISBN 0-8128-1756-6

I

The Late Swimmer

It was late in the year, I thought, for bathing, though there were still a few holidaymakers around, and for October it had been a pleasantly sunny day. But something made me think twice about the figure apparently sunbathing on the rocks. With a falling tide those rocks could be dangerous, some nasty little currents swirling round them. With the flood making as it was now they ought to be all right, but still I decided to take a closer look.

The wind was offshore and I'd been enjoying a long reach, aiming to clear Prawle Point before turning home for Salcombe. Now I put the yawl on the wind and stood in towards the clump of rocks masking the entrance to a cove I knew quite well. At low tide they would be uncovered, but now they were awash, and from the shore you would have to swim to get to them. As I got nearer, I saw that what I'd taken to be an indeterminate figure in a swimsuit was a woman, wearing not a swimsuit but a dress. She was lying very still—and what had been a pleasant afternoon seemed suddenly to turn cold.

With the plate down, the yawl drew some four feet six inches. I reckoned that there was probably a good fathom of water round the rocks; the incoming tide had a considerable swell, and waves were breaking on them. I dared not go too close, but I knew that somehow I had to get to the woman lying there. The only thing to do was to go in. I sailed past the rocks, let go the sheets, lifted the plate and anchored in about two feet of water. Then I took off my shoes and socks and went over the side, taking a line with me, and waded towards the rocks. As I had thought, I had to swim the last few yards. I discovered afterwards that I tore my shirt and gave my left ribs a painful graze in scrambling up, but I noticed neither then. All that mattered was to get to the woman.

As soon as I reached her I could see that she was dead. She was face-down on the rock, a green woollen dress clinging pathetically to what in life must have been quite an attractive body. She had stockings, but no shoes. I debated what to do. There seemed little enough that I could do *for* her, because I was sure that she was dead. But I could not be absolutely certain, and with the waves lapping over us I could not do anything where we were. I had to get her ashore.

I put the line I was carrying under her arms and round her shoulders and then, still holding the line, I half-slid, half-lifted her into the sea. Holding her to me, I swam on my back the few strokes that took me back into my depth. Then I carried her up the beach and put her down a few yards beyond the line of wrack that marked the normal reach of the tide. The little cove was quite deserted.

When I could look at her more closely it was obvious not only that she was dead, but that she had been dead, perhaps for a few days. One side of her face was badly battered, as if it had been banged repeatedly against the rocks. Her hair seemed dark because it was sodden, but where the wind had caught and dried a little tendril it looked as if it had once been fair. She seemed pitifully young, not more than in her early twenties. She wore no rings, but had a thin gold locket-chain round her neck. The chain was broken, and there was no locket; the chain had stayed on her because it was caught in the neck of her dress.

There is a coastguard station on Prawle Point and that

seemed the nearest place to go for help. It was some way, and a formidable climb to get to the cliff path. I couldn't carry her up by myself, so she would have to stay where she was while I climbed the cliff. I straightened her dress, and folded her arms gently. It couldn't matter at all to her, and I don't remember asking myself why I did it—respect for death is instinctive, I suppose. I put my wet handkerchief over her battered face, and it looked a little as if she were lying asleep.

I was beginning to shiver in my wet clothes, so the sooner I set off, the better. But I had to see to the yawl before I left. With her plate up she would take the ground quite happily, so I just pulled her in until she grounded, and laid out her anchor; with the tide coming in she would be afloat again before I could get back. I recovered my shoes and socks from the boat, and was glad that I should have dry feet for the climb.

I did not have to climb the whole way to the coastguard station, for I met the coastguard coming down. Sea and shore may seem utterly deserted, but it is surprising how little can happen without somebody's noticing. I knew the coastguard slightly, for I had often walked to Prawle Point, and had chatted with him occasionally. He was a big, friendly man, who had spent half a lifetime at sea. Now his kindly eyes were worried.

"Trouble?" he asked.

I told him what had happened.

"Aye," he said, "I thought I saw something on those rocks. Tide must have brought her in." Then he looked at me. "Are you quite sure she's dead?"

I said that I was quite sure.

"Then there's no purpose in your coming down again right away," he said. "Go on up to the station, and you'll find some dry clothes in the locker. And ring Kingsbridge

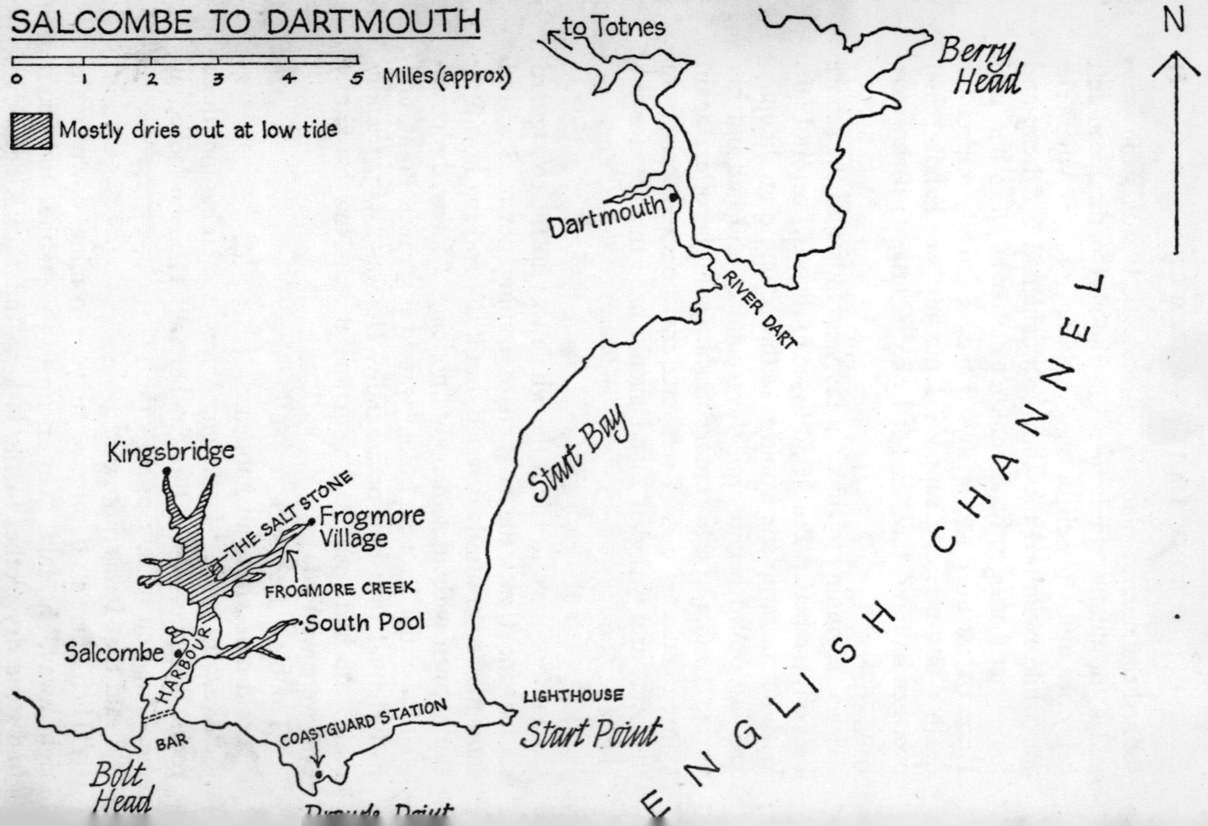
SALCOMBE TO DARTMOUTH
0 1 2 3 4 5 Miles (approx)
Mostly dries out at low tide
N
to Totnes
Berry Head
Dartmouth
RIVER DART
Start Bay
ENGLISH CHANNEL
LIGHTHOUSE
Start Point
Kingsbridge
THE SALT STONE
Frogmore Village
FROGMORE CREEK
South Pool
Salcombe
HARBOUR
BAR
COASTGUARD STATION
Bolt Head

police—the number's on the wall by the phone. There's a flask of tea on the shelf. Give yourself a hot drink, and wait out of the wind until the police come. I'll go down to the girl—and keep an eye on your boat."

I did as he said, but I thought I'd better telephone the police before I looked for dry clothes. I got through at once, and spoke to the station sergeant. He was concerned, but matter of fact: drowning, alas, is not uncommon. "We'll need ropes and a stretcher to get her up," he said, "but if she's dead there'll be no call for an ambulance. We can take her to the mortuary in a police van. The doctor will have to see her, though, before we move her. Can you wait at the coastguard station until our men come? It will save a lot of time if you show us just where she is."

I said that I'd certainly wait, and he promised that people would come as soon as they could.

That done, I had time to feel cold, and was conscious of pain from the scrape along my side. It was all superficial, though. I treated the graze with some ointment from the First Aid box, and gave myself a drink from the coastguard's flask of tea. It went down well. I found some trousers and a pullover in the locker, and although both were on the large side I changed into them.

It was the best part of an hour before the police came, but that was good going, and I'd expected to wait longer. To get to the Prawle cliffs from Kingsbridge they had first to get round Frogmore Creek at Frogmore, where I lived, and then take the narrow winding lanes to East Prawle. The road goes a mile or so beyond East Prawle, but there is no road right to the cliff, so the last part of the journey had to be on foot.

Four men came, a constable and police driver, both in uniform, a plain-clothes man whom I took to be a detective, and the doctor. The constable opened his notebook and introduced himself.

"Police Constable Murray," he said, "and my colleague is Detective-Sergeant Manning. This is Dr Robson. May I have your name, sir, please?"

"Peter James Blair," I said.

He wrote it down. "Address?"

"Rivermouth Cottage, Frogmore."

The detective-sergeant broke in.

"I think," he said, "that Mr Blair might make his statement later. It won't stay light for much longer, and we want to get the body up before dark. Would you show us the way, please, Mr Blair?"

It was not possible to walk two abreast on the cliff path, so I went first, followed by the detective-sergeant and the doctor. The constable and the police driver, carrying a folded canvas stretcher, a blanket and two coils of rope brought up the rear. Downhill it did not take long. The coastguard heard us coming, and was waiting at the foot of the cliff to meet us.

"You'll be glad of the dry clothes," he said to me.

"And the tea. Thank you very much," I said.

The girl was lying as I had left her. The coastguard had pulled in the yawl as the tide rose, and she was peacefully at anchor a few yards away. He had handed the sails, and put them tidily in their bags. The doctor went at once to the girl.

He removed my handkerchief, and stood for a moment just looking at her face. Then he knelt down, and examined the bruising that ran from her right temple down her cheek.

"Poor kid," he said. Then he stood up, and went on, "There's nothing I can do here. There'll have to be an autopsy, of course, but you can take her away now, Sergeant Manning."

"Could you give a rough idea, doctor, how long she has been dead?" asked the detective.

The doctor shrugged. "Anybody's guess," he said, "when a body's been in the sea. More than one day, certainly, but not much more. Say forty-eight hours or thereabouts. I can give you a better idea after the autopsy, but don't count on any great accuracy. These things are notoriously difficult."

The detective turned to me, "Where exactly did you find her, sir?" he asked.

I pointed to the group of rocks, now almost covered. "On the most seaward of those rocks," I said. "I think it's quite covered now, but you can't see it very well from the shore, anyway. I came in from the sea."

He nodded.

"Anything on the beach? Shoe, handbag, anything?"

"Nothing that I could see. There's the little chain on her neck."

He bent down, and gently took it off. "Lucky it caught in her dress," he said, "or it would be at the bottom of the sea. Not that it's of much value. Might just help to identify her, though." He took an envelope from his pocket and slipped the chain inside.

"Well, wherever she went in, it wasn't here," he went on. "We'd better get her up the cliff."

I thought about my boat. I couldn't get home in her now, because the tide was nearly full, and by the time I got back to the estuary I'd be meeting the ebb. That didn't matter so much, though it would make it hard to beat in, but by the time I got to Frogmore Creek there wouldn't be enough water for us. Almost all the inlet leading up to Frogmore dries out.

The men had wrapped the body in their blanket, and were strapping it to the stretcher. I explained about my boat. "Can you give me a lift to Frogmore?" I asked.

"Yes, of course," said the detective-sergeant. "We'll want a statement from you, anyway. Perhaps you'd give it to us at your house."

"Your boat will be all right here," the coastguard said.

"It's well sheltered, and I reckon the wind will stay offshore for tonight."

"Oh, yes, she'll be safe enough. I'll walk over and sail her round tomorrow," I answered. "And thank you for looking after her, and handing her sails."

The coastguard thought of something else. "To catch the flood going in to Salcombe, you'll be wanting to take her out on the last of the ebb," he said. "If she stays where she is, she won't be afloat then. I'll come down in the morning and anchor her out for you."

From the cove to the top of the cliff, where the path ran, there wasn't really a path at all. There was a rough track from boulder to boulder where people clambered down in summer, and it was excessively steep. The police put ropes on the stretcher, and with so much manpower available they got it up without much difficulty. Once on the path it could be carried normally.

A police van and two cars were parked at the end of the road. The body was put in the van, and it was arranged that the constable should go with it to the mortuary, while the detective-sergeant took me home. "I'll take Mr Blair's statement," the detective said. The van went off first. The doctor had come in his own car, and after promising a report on the autopsy as soon as he could get it done, he followed the van.

The detective lighted a pipe. "Whereabouts in Frogmore do you live?" he asked.

"A very small cottage," I said, "but it's been there about four hundred years, and you may know it. It's a bit out of the village, not far from the old mill. It was a fisherman's cottage for most of its history, but the last proper fisherman to live there died before the war. He was a widower, with a married daughter living in Plymouth. She didn't want the cottage, and my father bought it for holidays when I was about four or five."

"Worth a lot more now," the detective observed.

"Maybe. But I don't use it for holidays; it's the only home I've got," I said.

From East Prawle to Frogmore is only about four miles, but it was getting dusk, and no one can drive fast in those twisty, switchback lanes. The ride back took about twenty minutes. We didn't talk much in the car. I kept thinking of the girl, wondering who she was, and how she'd come to end up in the sea.

My cottage is almost on the road; it has about an acre of garden with a couple of sheds. My father had turned one of them into a garage, and made a side entrance to get to it. I had no car but that summer I'd started making a few chairs and tables for sale, simple cottage furniture, and I'd made a little gravelled parking place in front of the garage for people who stopped to have a look at them. The detective-sergeant put his car there, and we went into the cottage.

"Nice place," he said. Then, "Lord, what a lot of books!"

My books, some of them my father's, were about all I'd managed to save from the crash. There weren't really all that many, but I suppose in my tiny sitting-room they did seem rather a lot.

"I can't offer you a drink," I said, "because I haven't got one. But you're welcome to a cup of coffee. I'm going to make one for myself."

I put on the kettle, and the detective took out his notebook. "I'm sorry to trouble you," he said, "but I'm afraid we shall want as full a statement as you can make—everything you can remember."

I said that I understood, and he began to write. "Peter James Blair, I think you said." I nodded. "Address I've also got," he went on. "Profession?"

"Carpenter," I said.

He looked up, puzzled. "Have you always been a carpenter?"

"No, not really. But you don't want my life history. I'm a carpenter now, call it cabinet-maker, if you like—I make furniture." Then the kettle boiled, and I busied myself making the coffee. I was grateful for the interruption. I poured out two cups of coffee, and the detective did not pursue his investigation into me. I explained that the yawl had been my father's, and that sailing and walking were my chief recreations. Tide and wind had been just right today for a sail to Prawle. I'd almost got to the Point and was thinking of turning back when I noticed the girl on the rocks and sailed in to investigate.

"Why did you do that?" he asked.

"I don't really know," I said. "There are not many swimmers about at this time of year, and I suppose it seemed odd that she should be lying on the rock. As soon as I got close enough to see that she was wearing a dress and not a swimsuit I knew that something was wrong."

"Did you think of leaving her on the rock while you got help?"

"She couldn't have been left on the rock—the tide was coming in, and she would have been swept off it. And I didn't know where she might fetch up. There are all sorts of eddies round those rocks, and round Prawle Point. She wouldn't necessarily have come ashore in the cove. Besides, I couldn't be absolutely certain that she was dead. When I got her ashore I knew that she was past help, but I couldn't know until then."

"You have no idea who she is—was, I mean?"

"None whatever."

The detective shut his notebook.

"You did very well," he said, "and I'm sorry that your rescue-effort was no use. We shall have to set about trying to identify her. You'll be wanted at the inquest, I'm afraid, but you'll get notice of that. Well, thank you very much, Mr Blair."

The local West of England news on the radio next morning reported the finding of an unidentified dead woman on the rocks below Prawle Point, and there was a paragraph in the *Western Morning News*—I was described as "a local yachtsman". I didn't particularly want to be at home for possible reporters, and in any case I wanted to bring back my boat. I walked over to Prawle, and returned the coastguard's pullover and trousers. He had been as good as his word, and when I got down to the cove I found the yawl anchored well out, and comfortably afloat. I enjoyed the sail home. Going in to Salcombe I met another yawl coming out —she was *Princess Charming,* a new boat that had turned up during the summer. She was sailed by a rather bald man in gold-rimmed glasses—I'd seen him about before. Now he had a girl with him. We waved to each other as we passed. One of the joys of the Salcombe yawl is that she is not merely a fair-weather dinghy. She is descended from a long line of fishing boats, bred for these Devon waters and embodying the experience and skill of generations of men who have earned a living from the sea. Her little bowsprit makes her seem rather longer than she is, for she is only a sixteen-foot boat. For all her modest size, though, she is remarkably tough, and her small mizzen helps to keep her safe and controllable in a blow. Naturally, there is most sailing at Salcombe in the summer, but there are always a few boats in commission the year round and the traditional yawl is among the best of them. My own boat, *Lisa,* was getting on for twenty years old, but my father had kept her beautifully, and although it was only in the past year that I'd been able to sail her much, I'd managed to keep her looked after since he died. In appearance, at least, there wasn't much to choose between my boat and the new yawl that I'd passed, and I reckoned that the new boat would do well to come up to mine in sailing qualities. I wondered for a moment at his going out against the tide, but then I thought that probably he had a mooring in the harbour, and so could get back when he wanted to.

The dead girl was soon identified, though in a curious way. No one seemed to know anything about her locally, so the police began the rounds of hotels and boarding houses in the Kingsbridge–Salcombe–Totnes area. At the second hotel they went to in Salcombe they were lucky. No, said the manager when given a description of the girl, he'd had no one staying there who could possibly fit, but he was getting a little concerned about a guest who had not turned up. He showed the police two letters from a Miss Edna Brown. She had written from an address at Earl's Court, London, about three weeks earlier asking if there was a single room available for the third week of October. The manager had replied saying that there was, and she had then written to book it. In her second letter she explained that she would be spending part of her holiday on a walking tour on Dartmoor, and would be coming to Salcombe for the last week. She did not want luggage on the walking tour, so she had asked a friend who was driving to South Devon to deliver a suitcase for her to the hotel. This would be on a Saturday or Sunday, and she herself would follow on the Monday. Would the hotel please look after the suitcase until she came?

A polite note that the hotel would be delighted to do so concluded the correspondence. The suitcase had duly arrived, but Miss Brown had not. This was now a week ago, and the manager was beginning to be worried about payment for the room. On learning this the police decided to have a look at the suitcase. It was locked, but the lock was so flimsy that a penknife quickly had it open. It was packed with a bundle of old newspapers, and on top of the papers was a letter addressed "To Whom It May Concern". This was read at the inquest, and the sad little story was explained.

The coroner took evidence of identification first. The dead girl appeared to have no known relatives, and she was identified by a Miss Bunty Wilberforce, with whom she shared a flat at the Earl's Court address, and by a Mr Angus Potterton, director of an advertising agency for which she had worked as a shorthand typist for nearly two years. Her age, obtained from the records of the Department of Health and Social Security via her National Insurance number was just under twenty-two.

Mr Potterton was a surprise. He gave a London address, but he was undoubtedly the man I'd seen sailing *Princess Charming*. Though why shouldn't an advertising man have a boat at Salcombe? He might have clients in South Devon, for all I knew. And it was no business of mine.

I was called next, and repeated my statement of how I had found the body.

Then came the medical evidence. Death was due to drowning. There were severe injuries to her forehead and face, but these could have been caused after death, and were consistent with her being thrown by the sea against rocks. An autopsy had shown that she was about three months pregnant.

The letter from the suitcase was read by the coroner. It was typed, with a handwritten signature. The letter said:

I suppose somebody will read this some day, but I don't care if nobody ever does. I'm not wanted, anyway. When I told him that I was going to have a baby, he didn't want to know. He just said that I could get an abortion on the Health Service. Well, I suppose I could have got an abortion, but if my baby has got to be killed, I want to go, too. I know exactly what to do. I'm going to walk into the sea when the tide is going out, and when it gets deep I shall just let the sea take me. Then nobody will have to bother about burying me.

Miss Brown had had a bank account, with a credit balance of £185.35. The signature on the letter agreed with the specimen signature held by the bank.

Miss Wilberforce and Mr Potterton, recalled, both said that they knew nothing of Miss Brown's condition, and neither could offer any suggestion as to who might be the man referred to in her letter. "Edna was very attractive," Miss Wilberforce said, "and she used to go out a lot. Boy friends were always ringing her up. But she didn't have people at the flat, so I don't know any of them."

The coroner was a kindly man. In a brief address to the jury he said that the letter, taken in conjunction with the evidence of where and how the body was found, might well seem to justify a verdict of suicide. But the jury would bear in mind that the unfortunate Miss Brown was pregnant, and that women in pregnancy—particularly in Miss Brown's situation—might often suffer some form of mental disturbance. It was, of course, a matter for the jury, but he felt that in all the circumstances they might reasonably conclude that she had taken her own life while the balance of her mind had been disturbed.

The jury found this entirely reasonable, and returned a verdict accordingly. I felt that the sea had rather let her down. She had wanted to slip out of the world quietly, leaving no mess for anybody to clear up, but she had come back to the land, causing a lot of trouble to a lot of people. Just before the court rose, Mr Potterton stood up. He gave a polite little cough, took off his glasses and polished them for a moment with his handkerchief. Then he said that as there appeared to be no relatives, his agency would be happy to pay for the girl's funeral. The coroner observed that that was most generous, and said he was sure that the police would readily concur with Mr Potterton's suggestion.

Although sensational enough in its way, the inquest on Miss Brown did not get much space in the national papers. It coincided with cliff-hanging attempts to settle a threatened national railway strike, and the deposition of the president of an African state by a group of officers in his Army, with much resulting turmoil, and several British journalists clapped in gaol. One paper, which had been running an anti-abortion campaign, had a short, moralising leader about one girl's preference for death rather than abortion, and that was that.

Two days after the inquest my cottage was burgled. And two days after that, I was blown up.

2

The Letter-bomb

BURGLARY AND LETTER-BOMBS leave one feeling shaken and confused. I will set out what happened as clearly as I can, though some of my recollections are a bit hazy. The burglary first—I'm clear enough about that. It happened at about four o'clock in the morning. My cottage is not difficult to get into: I do not bolt the door, and it can be opened easily enough by putting an arm through a window in the porch—I have done this several times myself when I have forgotten the key. The prowling thief is not a country character, and having little worth stealing it had never occurred to me to take any particular precautions against thieves. Old cottages are given to odd grunts and groans in the night, but I was familiar with the noises of mine and they did not disturb me. When I woke suddenly that morning, I knew at once that there was something wrong. I lay very still, listening, and I was sure that I could hear someone moving about stealthily downstairs. My bedroom door, opening, as in most cottages, straight from the top of the stairs, does not fit well, and I caught the flash of a torch underneath it. I got up as quickly as I could, then flung open the door and rushed downstairs. I was hoping to take whoever it was by surprise, but I was not quite quick enough—he was out of the front door before I could get down. I saw a dim figure running down the road; he was going as fast as he could and had such a start that it seemed pretty hopeless to go after him. In any case, I was in pyjamas, and not dressed for a cross-country chase. Also, I wanted to know what had happened in the cottage.

There is only one sitting-room, and it was in an appalling mess. Every drawer in my desk was open, with the contents just scattered about the floor. Books had been taken from the shelves, and added to the confusion on the floor. My most valuable possessions, a pair of Georgian silver candlesticks, had not been touched.

I had no telephone in the cottage, but there is a call-box in the road about fifty yards away. I got dressed, and went there to telephone the police at Kingsbridge. The duty officer asked for a description of the man. There wasn't much that I could give him. He said that he would get in touch with the patrol car nearest to me by radio and that somebody would come as soon as possible.

I went back to the cottage and made coffee. In about twenty minutes a police car did come, and I told my story to a sympathetic policeman. He looked at the mess in my sitting room and asked me to disturb it as little as I could so that it could be examined later by an officer of the CID. He wanted to know what had been taken, but I said that I couldn't know until I'd sorted out the mess. I added that as far as I could see, nothing had been taken, and there wasn't much of any value to take, except the candlesticks, and they seemed to be all right.

"Ah," he said, "then it looks as if you disturbed him in time. Well, sir, I'll get the CID to come along, but unless they can find fingerprints of someone we know, I'm afraid there isn't much that we can do."

My old acquaintance, Detective-Sergeant Manning, came soon after nine o'clock. "You again, sir," he said cheerfully. "What a mess!"

When he saw how easily the window by the door had been forced, he gave me a lecture about asking for trouble. "Endless police time could be saved, and people could save themselves a lot of misery, if only they'd lock doors and windows properly," he said.

He obviously considered the burglary largely my own fault, but he went about his investigation thoroughly. The rough woodwork of an old cottage offers few good surfaces for fingerprints, but the polished top of my desk, he thought, might show something. He dusted it with a fine powder, and, sure enough, several fingerprints showed up. Most were pretty smudgy, but one was reasonably clear. He photographed them all carefully, and then said, "Of course, they may turn out to be yours. May I have a set of your prints for comparison?" He took a small inked pad from his case, and made prints from my fingers and thumbs of both hands. I'd been through this before, in the days when you had to be fingerprinted to get a visa to visit the United States.

He studied the best print on my desk, and remarked, "Offhand, I'd say it probably was one of yours. But they'll go to Exeter to be examined by an expert."

He helped me to go through the mess on the floor. My cheque-book was intact, and two £1 notes, which had been in the same drawer, were on the floor with it.

"Whoever it was didn't seem to want money," he said. "But he was looking for something. Are you sure you don't know what it was?"

I said that I had absolutely no idea. As far as I knew I possessed nothing, except, perhaps, the silver candlesticks, that anyone would want to steal.

He was with me for nearly an hour and a half. He wrote down my statement recounting the events of the night—I was getting used to making police statements—and went away.

I tidied up, and then walked into Kingsbridge to buy some bolts. It seemed a good example of locking the stable after the departure of the horse, but I was more upset than I would have admitted—it is a vile feeling that somebody, presumably malign, has been going through all one's possessions. I fitted bolts to the door and all the downstairs windows. My cottage has no back door, and I thought that if its one door and its windows were securely bolted it would be difficult for the burglar to stage a repeat performance.

Nothing happened that night, or the next night. I was reluctant to be away from the cottage, so I stayed at home during the day, getting on with a set of chairs I was making in my workshop-shed. I didn't think it likely that anyone would try to break in by day, but I kept the windows bolted, and I locked the door every time I went from the cottage to the shed. It was a great nuisance, and I wondered for how long I'd have the patience to go on doing it.

On the second morning after the burglary, the postman brought me three letters. One was an electricity bill, and one a letter from a man who had bought a table and four chairs from me a month or so back, asking if I could make two more chairs to bring his set to six. The third was a smallish packet rather than a letter, a fat envelope with a typed address, like the circulars one gets enclosing a bundle of order-forms and leaflets. I opened it without much interest, and woke up in hospital.

My survival was a credit to my own workmanship. The letters came when I was having breakfast, and I was sitting at a table that I'd made myself. I must have been sitting back a bit, away from the table, when I opened the letter, and the table took the main force of the explosion. The wood was cracked, but did not shatter: it saved my legs and the lower part of my body. My chair and I were thrown across the room, but my head hit nothing worse than books. The other letters apparently caught fire, and some burning bits were flung against the window curtains, setting them alight. The windows were blown out.

My cottage stands by itself, but there is a row of cottages

almost opposite, and there are more houses a little down the road. People heard the explosion and rushed out. Mercifully, I'd unbolted the door when I opened it for the postman, and I was dragged out before the fire got much of a hold. The fire itself was put out with buckets of water from the cottages across the way. A neighbour telephoned from the call-box for fire brigade and ambulance. There was little for the firemen to do when they came, for the fire was then out, but they inspected the beams to make sure that nothing was left smouldering.

I knew nothing of all this at the time, for I was still unconscious when the ambulance arrived. I came to in hospital, and soon afterwards my old friend Detective-Sergeant Manning was brought in by a nurse. He wanted yet another statement, and the nurse said that I could make one if I felt well enough. I was still pretty confused; all I could say was that I remembered opening a letter and nothing else at all.

I got off extraordinarily lightly. I was badly shocked and bruised, some of my hair was singed, and I had a painful burn on one cheek, but nothing was broken, and no lasting damage seemed to have been done. After a day in bed in hospital I wanted to get up, but they wouldn't let me, saying that I'd have to stay in bed for at least another two or three days. I did, however, have a visitor. He came around midday on my second day in hospital and began to introduce himself as Detective Chief Superintendent Payne. I say "began to introduce himself" because he'd got out the Superintendent bit when he said, "Lord, Peter Blair." I recognised him too. "It's good to see you, George," I said. "But what on earth brings you here?"

"I belong to the Devon CID at Exeter," he said. "We thought that you were getting a bit accident-prone."

"First lecture—Intelligence Course at Aldershot. Putting two and two together."

"And making five." We both laughed.

George sat down beside the bed. "But I didn't know it was you," he said.

There wasn't any reason why he should have connected me with the Blair who kept on drawing police attention to himself in a small South Devon village. We'd been subalterns together in the Army, but that was a long time ago. We both belonged to that rather lost half-generation which had been too young to fight in the war but old enough to remember it, old enough, too, to be caught up in military service. "Caught up", though, is hardly the right term to use about myself. All the time I was at school I accepted that everyone became a soldier if he could, and I went from school to Sandhurst as what seemed to me a matter of course. George had a National Service Commission. But we'd known each other as boys before we met again in the Army. My father was a doctor in Ashburton, and George's father, like his son a policeman, had been stationed there until he was promoted and transferred to Bideford. His family were all my father's patients—I daresay my father brought George into the world.

George left the Army when his term of National Service was up and joined the police. He had obviously done well, though at the time I was sorry to see him go, and had tried to persuade him to stay on. As a regular officer, I was committed to the Army, but it turned out that the Army wasn't quite so committed to me. I'd just got my majority when my regiment was amalgamated with two others, and there were three majors for every major's job. I might have survived, but I was sickened by the whole business and decided to pack up. Construction Industries Investments, the big combine marketing every sort of building material and equipment, was at that time recruiting ex-officers, and gave me a job. I worked hard, or was lucky, or both, for within five years I was General Sales Manager for the whole concern. I earned what seemed to me a great deal of money, married Sybil, bought a splendid house in Chelsea, and seemed set for the chairmanship and an eventual knighthood. Then Construction Industries Investments was taken over by Amalgamated Suppliers, and at forty-three I was out of a job. I'd never thought about negotiating any special contract with the firm for myself, and it appeared that I was still employed on the terms on which I had joined, which provided for three months' notice. I was given six months' pay, which the new chairman seemed to consider generous. "A sort of leaden handshake," I remember saying when he told me.

"I read about your father's death in the local paper," George was saying. "They thought a lot of him in Ashburton. Would it be four, or five years ago? He wasn't very old."

"No, he was not quite sixty-four," I said. "He never retired. After my mother died he worked all the hours God sends. It was good for the patients, I suppose, but it killed him. I often wish now that I gone in for medicine, so that I could have helped in the practice. He would have liked that, really. But probably it wouldn't have worked—I'm not cut out to be a doctor. Is your father still alive?"

"Oh yes, and my mother. Both still pretty active, and still living near Bideford."

I thought what a mess I'd made of my life compared with George Payne.

"Peter, are you well enough to talk?" he said.

"Oh yes, if you want to."

"Well, I do. You've given the police a lot to think about."

"I've had a lot to think about as well."

"You realise that we've had to make inquiries about you?"

I hadn't realised that, because I hadn't thought about it.

Looking at things now from the police point of view, I saw that I must have seemed a rather odd character.

"I'm sorry," I said.

"We discovered that you'd lost your job, that your wife left you about eighteen months ago and you came to live at Frogmore and that you were divorced about six months ago. Is this very painful, Peter?"

"Not particularly now," I said. "I don't even blame Sybil any longer; I understand things a bit better. She is very attractive and very expensive, a sort of natural whore—quite a lot of women are, you know, and some of the nicest of them. She has what men want, or think they want, and she's eager to sell, but she sets a high price. As long as I was earning plenty of money, able to give her all the clothes and things she wanted, and to take her to the right parties, we were fine. She even looked after me, in a way, but I see now that she was protecting my earning capacity rather than me. When I couldn't pay what she expected, it was no good. She went off with the man who took my job—sort of winner takes all."

"But why did you call yourself a carpenter? If you'd said 'Major Blair' it would have saved us a lot of trouble. And I'd have come to see you straight away."

"Because, dammit, I *am* a carpenter. When the crash came and Sybil left me, I had a good look at myself, and I didn't like what I saw. I'd lived soft, and I *was* soft. And I didn't have much money. With Sybil to keep I'd lived up to the hilt, over the hilt, and I'd put nothing by. Inflation added about £20,000 to the house, but there was a huge mortgage, and when that was paid off, and the other bills paid, there was about £12,000 left. Half of that had to go to Sybil. So I had £6,000—all due to inflation—to show for my years as a tycoon. I had about £10,000 left of what I'd inherited from my father, and the cottage at Frogmore. Thank God that wasn't reckoned part of the matrimonial home, so I was able to keep it. I wanted to sort myself out. With capital of about £16,000 I wasn't exactly on the breadline. But I'd been earning that in a year. I wanted to prove to myself that I didn't need it. My £16,000, invested timidly but safely, brings in a little over £20 a week. I used to spend twice that on taking Sybil out to dinner. Now I've found that I can live on it, and live quite well.

"You knew my father, George, and you may remember that he had three great interests in life—medicine, sailing Salcombe yawls, and woodworking. He was always wonderful with his hands. I didn't inherit the interest in medicine, but I did inherit the other two—and I inherited his tools. When I was a tycoon I hadn't time for carpentering; Sybil would have thought it messy, anyway. When I got to the cottage it was sheer joy to handle tools again, and it did me a lot of good. I didn't have much furniture, so I made myself a table and a set of chairs. Some time back a man stopped to ask the way to Prawle. My door opens into the sitting-room, so he came in. He saw the table, asked if I knew who made it, and said he'd pay £50 for one just like it. Well, the wood had cost me about £12, so it seemed a reasonable profit on my labour. I made him a table, and then he asked for a set of chairs, so I made those, too. I enjoyed the work, and it struck me that there might be a market for it, so I made some more and turned what had been the garage into a sort of showroom. I suppose people driving around on holiday haven't really much to do, for quite a lot of them stop to have a look at my stuff, and I've made nearly £400 this summer. Next year I shall do better, for I shall be better organised, and in the winter I can make for stock. I can't tell you what a relief it is to know that I can make a living with my hands."

George was quiet for what seemed a long time. Then he said, "If you're alive next summer."

I was startled—I don't think I'd really taken in the events

of the past week. "You mean, whoever had a go at me with the bomb will try again?"

He nodded. "Yes, I mean just that—unless we can find out who it is and stop him. There wasn't much left of your bomb, Peter, but there was enough for the forensic people to find out that it was a professional and very nasty piece of work. *Someone* has it in for you, and we've just *got* to know who. Did you discover what was stolen when you were burgled?"

"Nothing was stolen," I said.

"That's what you thought, Peter, but you were wrong. Sergeant Manning is a very able chap. You had a pile of photograph frames on one of your bookshelves."

"Yes, but they were only frames. They'd had mostly pictures of Sybil. I couldn't face keeping the pictures, but I kept the frames—I hardly ever throw away a piece of wood."

"Well, you may have thought they were all empty, but they weren't. One of them had had a photograph of you. It had been torn out hurriedly and clumsily, and Sergeant Manning noticed a bit of the cardboard mount left in the frame. By a stroke of luck it had the photographer's name on it—very posh photographer, too, Peter. We asked the Metropolitan Police to try to find out what the photograph was, and since we could give them your name as well as the photographer's they got it almost at once. It was a photograph of you, taken to accompany a news story sent out by your public relations people when you got some huge order for British cement from one of the Arab oil states in the Middle East."

"Sure, I remember now. The PR people gave me a framed copy of the photograph, and I gave it to Sybil. Obviously she didn't want to take it with her. I must have collected it with the other frames, and I suppose I didn't bother to take out that particular photograph. I can't say one way or the other."

"Well, it *was* torn out, and presumably by your burglar. I say by your burglar, because it was *torn* out, and all the other frames had had their pictures taken out neatly. Do you see what that means, Peter? Someone wants your photograph so badly that he's prepared to break into your home on the chance of finding one."

"Or of finding something else," I said.

"Yes, but what? You told Manning that you had nothing that anyone would want to steal. Who *is* this enemy of yours, Peter? Could your ex-wife's new husband want to kill you?"

I had to laugh at that. "Lord, no," I said. "He's got my job as well as Sybil—I'm no conceivable threat to him. I'm not saying that he may not find himself wishing sometimes that I'd take her back, but that's another matter. If *I'd* been trying to kill *him*, it might make sense. It makes no sense at all your way round."

"Rack your brains, Peter. Can you think of any enemy you may have made in business?"

"I suppose one does make enemies in business—if you get an order that someone else wants, he doesn't exactly love you for it. But this is happening all the time, and sales managers don't go round killing one another. Discontented customers for my furniture? As far as I know I haven't got any. If, say, a leg fell off one of my chairs—which it won't—but *if* it did —I'd expect the customer to demand a new chair, not to try to kill me. No, George, it's just plain lunacy."

"The bomb was real, and the burglary was real."

George got up and walked to the window and back. I was exasperated, and beginning to feel tired. George was an old friend, but I wished that he would go away. But what he was saying wouldn't go away. I pulled myself together, and said, "The only really out-of-the-way thing that's ever happened to me was finding that girl's body on the rocks. I can't think *why* anybody should regard it as my fault, but I think these extraordinary attacks on me *must* be connected with her in some way. There was a lot left unexplained at the inquest."

"There was a lot that didn't come out at all at the inquest," George said. He paused for a moment, then went on, "I suppose it's a bit irregular, but you're mixed up in the thing anyway, and I don't see why you shouldn't know what we think. You may even be able to help us. . .

"There was a good deal of evidence not given at that inquest, Peter. We didn't want more publicity than we'd got to have, and the coroner understood. First, we don't think that her name was Edna Brown. We *do* think that she was Gwen Rosing. Do you remember that great scandal about three years ago when a Cabinet Minister and some top Civil Servants were mixed up in what the papers called 'Love Nest in Whitehall'? The Rosing girl was the star of that rather nasty show and from all we were able to discover she was a vicious little kid. She was around eighteen then, which would make her about right for the age of the girl you found."

A little scene came back to me vividly—the wind's drying a tendril of her hair. "It won't do, George," I said. "Gwen Rosing was a brunette—surely you remember the papers calling her 'The Burning Brunette'. The girl I found was fair."

"No, Peter. She had fair hair, yes; but it was dark brown at the roots. She'd just turned herself into a blonde."

"But doesn't anybody know what happened to her. She was so famous, or infamous, that somebody is bound to know."

"That's just it, Peter, they don't. She is supposed to have gone to Canada or Australia. Did you read a series of nauseating articles in one of the Sunday papers, called 'I have learned my Lesson. All I want Now is to be a Wife and Mother'? They were written for her by some ghost, and their theme was that she was emigrating to make good. As far as we know she never left England, but she did disappear. And she disappeared so successfully that in spite of her notoriety and news-value she has not been heard of since.

"Now I must change tack a bit. About a year ago we began to notice a big increase in the amount of heroin being pushed by young undergraduates. It was noticed first in London, but soon afterwards at Oxford and Cambridge, and more recently we've come across it in Exeter. At least a dozen other universities are suffering in the same way, and although the pushers seem mostly undergraduates, of course they don't stop at selling in their universities. It's not difficult to run in some of the silly young fools who think it clever, or 'with it' to go round retailing drugs, but they're not the importers, and when they say they don't know the name of whoever they got it from, they're usually telling the truth. It's hard to make some of them realise that they're doing anything particularly wrong—an enormous amount of harm has been done by the apostles of permissiveness who try to suggest that cannabis and the other so-called 'soft' drugs don't really matter much. Get hooked on one, and it's not a long step to look for a new sensation in trying something else. And heroin isn't a 'soft' drug.

"The heroin we've been coming across lately isn't very pure heroin, though it's deadly enough. It's probably manufactured somewhere in the East, but how it's getting into this country in the quantities it obviously is, we simply don't know. We suspect that a new organisation has come on the scene, importing the stuff somehow, and distributing it very efficiently via these university students. One of the troubles is that heroin can be imported in very small parcels—in terms of value for weight it's about the most paying merchandise there is.

"The student-pushers are expendable. If they get caught—and, as I've said, we do catch them—they don't know enough to be dangerous to the importer. But there's got to be a link somewhere. We've been picking up rumours of a girl who's been going round universities, not, it seems, selling heroin herself, but letting people know where they can get it. And from three separate places have come suggestions that this girl is—or was—Gwen Rosing.

"To get back to the inquest. We've no doubt that the girl was using the name Edna Brown. She genuinely worked for that advertising agency, and she lived as Edna Brown where her flat-mate said she did. Since the very last thing we wanted was to draw attention to our knowledge of Gwen Rosing we felt that she might as well be buried as Edna Brown. But there was some other medical evidence that wasn't given— there was a recent mark from a hypodermic syringe on her arm. There were no indications that she herself had become an addict, but traces of heroin, and it was this particularly impure heroin, were found in her body.

"That was one thing. There was something else. You saw the bruising on her face, but I wonder if you remember the precise words of the medical evidence about it? Well, they were that the injuries '*could have been* caused' after death. The pathologist was on our side in agreeing not to give certain evidence at all, but he refused—and one can only respect him for it—to say anything that he felt to be actually untrue. He himself had grave doubts about those injuries, and he considered that she had been struck at least once—on her temple—before death. He did agree, however, that he couldn't be absolutely certain, and after a good deal of persuasion he accepted the formula saying '*could have been*'. As to the bit about the injuries being consistent with her head hitting and scraping a rock, that really meant nothing at all —of course your head will be hurt if it hits a rock. However, it gave the impression we wanted, and the pathologist didn't object.

"Now, do you see the significance of all this? If that girl was hit on the head before she died, given a shot of heroin and thrown in the sea, somebody wanted badly to get rid of her. You may say, why knock her out if she's going to have heroin?—Well, it's very hard to give an injection to somebody who's struggling against it. The blow and the heroin are reasonable enough. They are also clever: she would be unconscious when she was thrown in the sea, but she would be alive, and she had to be alive, otherwise she would not drown. And that would not have fitted in with the letter we were meant to find.

"If all, or even any, of this is true, you seem to be suspected of having seen something to suggest that the girl was not drowned in the way she's supposed to have been drowned. What this is I don't know, and I'm quite sure you don't know, but it's obviously something so dangerous to the people concerned—let's call them the Importers—that they are quite ready to kill you. We've got to think hard, *hard*, Peter. You can see why I'm so worried about you."

I wasn't tired any longer, but the nurse came in to send George away. "The doctor said that Mr Blair wasn't to have visitors," she said. "We only let you come in because you're the police. Mr Blair has had severe concussion, and now he must rest."

I said I didn't want to rest, but she was adamant. I won a concession that I should be allowed to say goodbye—she said she would come back in five minutes to show George out.

When she had gone, George said, "Look, Peter—your cottage is in a hell of a mess, and you can't go back there when you leave hospital. Will you come and stay with me? We've plenty of room, and I'd be a lot happier to have you with us rather than alone in that cottage. Apart from anything else, we *are* old friends."

I'd nowhere else to go. I thought it very nice of George, and said Yes, of course I'd come.

He was pleased, and relieved. "At least we can keep an eye on you," he said. "I'll be in touch with the hospital, and when they say you can come out I'll drive over to collect you. And I'm going to have a man on duty here until you leave. Country hospitals are not exactly high-security places, and I don't like to think how vulnerable you are. I'll tell the nurse to see that your window is kept bolted. Good luck."

The nurse wanted me to have dinner, but I said that I could not possibly eat anything, and I asked her to take the tray away. The idea that somebody was seriously out to kill me for some reason that I couldn't begin to fathom was so horrible that for a long time I just lay and looked at the ceiling, fearing that unless I lay still and clenched my hands hard I should be physically sick. Then I began to feel angry. Who was this bastard who'd broken into my house, and sent me a bomb by post? Of all cowardly and disgusting ways to kill, the letter-bomb is about the worst. The killer can't even be sure that the right person is going to be killed—there's a chance, and quite a high chance, that some utterly unrelated man, woman or child will be murdered, or maimed for life. Whoever was after me was certainly a coward; he'd run away when I disturbed him in my cottage, and instead of going after me himself he'd sent a bomb by post. If I could get my hands on him—well, I'd been quite good at what the Army calls unarmed combat.

Then I began to think over what George had been saying, and I got angrier still. The bastard after me didn't want to kill me for anything I'd done—he wanted me out of the way so that he could go on selling heroin to wreck the lives of God knew how many youngsters. They might be silly young fools, they might even be fairly evil young fools, but unless somebody pushed drugs at them they wouldn't start taking them. And there was the girl, Gwen Rosing. "A vicious young kid," George had said. Well, maybe. I remembered the

"Whitehall Love Nest" scandal very well: no one in Britain could possibly not remember it, for it had dominated press, television and the radio for weeks. The Rosing girl, and two or three other young prostitutes, had been installed in a Government flat in Whitehall with the connivance of a corrupt official of the Ministry of Architecture. He was paid, and the whole thing was financed, by a big property developer. The set-up formed a select and most superior brothel. When the developer had difficulty in getting planning permission for building on some property he'd bought, the Town Clerk, chairman of the Planning Committee, or other top boss of the local authority concerned, would be invited to an informal conference at the Ministry. They'd be invited to the flat for lunch or dinner. The whole thing was ostensibly quite respectable, the girls acting as waitresses. If it was obvious that the officials or aldermen being entertained were not corruptible, the party would end as respectably as it began. If, after a good deal to drink, hints of a possible good time were well received, the girls were ready to oblige. And at the most embarrassing moments photographs would be taken. So the developer added to his millions. The thing came unstuck when one Town Clerk who was being blackmailed shot himself, and left a letter for the police.

There was naturally a fearful scandal. The Minister of Architecture, who was probably guilty of no greater crime than failing to keep a close enough eye on his officials—he was never proved to have taken part in any of the goings-on at the flat—resigned from the Cabinet and applied for the Chiltern Hundreds. His political career, and he was in the running for the deputy-leadership of his party, was ruined. Two senior Civil Servants went to prison, and it was generally felt that several more ought to have gone. Two Town Clerks were dismissed, and struck off the roll of Solicitors, a Mayor committed suicide, and a number of aldermen had to resign from their respective councils. The property developer discreetly took himself off to South America, selecting a country with no extradition treaty with Britain. He was supposed to have masses of money salted away in Swiss banks.

The Rosing girl had been the hostess, or chief performer, at the flat. She was exceptionally pretty, and in various interviews she gave she seemed to be exceptionally intelligent. When the storm was at its height she was arrested for a few days, but nobody seemed to know what charge could be brought against her, and she was released. Her Sunday paper articles, after the Civil Servants had been sentenced, caused a fresh outburst, with several questions in Parliament asking why she was not herself in the dock. She had presumably taken part in a conspiracy; but could she claim that what was done with photographs of her in compromising positions was no concern of hers? The Government kept on saying that the Law Officers were considering her case, but the uncertainty dragged on for so long that newspapers began to express some sympathy for her as a child corrupted by a bunch of nasty old men. In the end the whole thing was dropped—no proceedings were ever brought against her. The Government evidently felt that the affair had had quite enough publicity, and she herself helped to bring the fuss to an end by lying low and saying nothing. Thinking back over it all now, I felt that her disappearance from the hundreds of reporters who had been hunting her was a considerable feat.

With everybody else, I'd argued the case endlessly at the time. Most women tended to be anti-Rosing, partly, one couldn't help feeling, because she was so pretty. Sybil, who feared no competition in that direction, was inclined to stick up for her, on the ground that it was the old story of Adam's running for cover and blaming Eve. My chief loathing was for the property developer, who had apparently made a lot of money, and got off scot free. I was particularly sorry for the Cabinet Minister, whose politics I had rather admired. Like other Nine Days' Wonders, the whole thing now seemed to belong to another world.

I thought back to the girl on the rocks: was she anything like what I could recall of the photographs of Gwen Rosing? Her battered face made it hard to say. And she was a bit older than the dewy eighteen-year-old whose picture had filled the papers. And she was dead. Her build was probably about right, but that could be said of thousands of young women. But if the police thought she was Gwen Rosing, she probably was.

What on earth could make me dangerous to her associates —now ex-associates? I'd done nothing whatever except find her body. It was all very well for George Payne to say that I *must* be in possession of some knowledge that I didn't know I had, but there wasn't any knowledge I *could* have. I'd reported the finding of the body. I'd given evidence at the inquest—there just wasn't anything else. I couldn't be expected to know of hypodermic syringe marks on her—I wouldn't recognise a hypodermic syringe mark, even if I'd noticed it. And I wouldn't know anything about it now, if George Payne hadn't told me. If he was right, and somebody had killed the girl, that somebody might well fear the police doctors, but there was no reason to fear me. And that somebody couldn't know that the police had decided not to disclose all the medical evidence. There'd been a perfectly normal inquest, a coroner's jury had been satisfied—no crime of any sort had even been hinted at. Whoever was involved —if anybody was involved—seemed to me to be sitting pretty. Everything had gone exactly as he hoped.

Then why try to kill me? Much as I should have preferred to think of my bomb as a bad dream, I couldn't reasonably pretend that it hadn't happened. The burglary had happened, too. George seemed to think that I'd been burgled for a photograph of myself but I couldn't really believe that. It would have been a lot of trouble and some risk for a most chancy result. How could the burglar know that he would find a photograph—I hadn't even known myself that there was a picture of me in the pile of old frames. I could see that *if* George was right, and if, say, No 1 Enemy wanted to hand over the task of dealing with me to Enemy No 2, a photograph would be useful, almost necessary. (Though the sender of the bomb hadn't bothered much about who would actually get it.) But there are easier ways of getting hold of a photograph than breaking into someone's house: why not hang around with a camera, and take a picture of me coming out? No, whoever broke into the cottage was looking for something definite that I was supposed to have; something to do with the girl, which ought to have been mentioned at the inquest but wasn't, and which, therefore, was presumably still in my possession, because I hadn't reported it to the police. The missing photograph could be explained simply: the thief came across it and took it on the spur of the moment, reckoning that it might come in useful. He had not set out to look for my photograph.

But what? The girl was wearing a simple one-piece dress, of some greenish fabric. I hadn't examined it at all closely. Did it have sleeves? I concentrated on trying to remember. No, it certainly hadn't had long sleeves, because her arms were bare, but it might have had short sleeves, just covering the top of her arms—that would explain why I hadn't noticed any scratch or syringe-mark, though I didn't think I'd have thought twice about it if I had. I couldn't remember seeing any sort of pocket on her dress. She had no handbag, and as far as I knew none had been washed ashore. She hadn't even had a wrist-watch.

I remembered the little gold chain round her neck. It couldn't possibly be that. It had gone off with her body to the mortuary, and it was broken, anyway. It could not have much value—it might not even be gold. There was nothing else; there just was *nothing* that I could conceivably have taken.

I went on turning things over and over in my mind, coming to no conclusion, except an ever-growing conviction that it was all some weird mistake.

When the nurse came in I realised that the whole afternoon had gone. "I hope you had a nice sleep," she said brightly. "Would you like some supper?"

I didn't enlighten her. I said that I thought I could manage a cup of soup. She brought this, and then I had to have some medicine. It must have been a fairly powerful sedative, for in spite of everything on my mind I slept dreamlessly until morning.

3
The Locket

THREE DAYS AFTER George's visit I was discharged. George came for me as he had promised, and drove me first to the cottage to collect some clothes. Poor cottage—my neighbours had been very kind and had done their best to clean up, but the explosion, fire and water had left a dreadful mess. The downstairs windows were blown out, huge chunks of plaster had been torn from the walls, and there was a hole in the ceiling. I was relieved to see, though, that, as with me, the damage was really only superficial. The thick stone walls behind the plaster were as solid as ever, and the old beams had taken the bomb as merely an incident in the centuries since they had been oak-trees.

"I'd like to get the windows mended, or at least boarded up," I said. "And the plaster has got to be renewed. If it's at all possible, I'd like to get it done while I'm away."

George approved. "It will be a good idea to let people know that you are going away," he said. "But be a bit vague —don't give an address."

Mrs Moss, across the road, was a kindly soul, and I suspected that she had done most of the cleaning up. I went over to thank her; she seemed genuinely pleased to see me up and about again. "Oh, Mr Blair, what a dreadful business," she said. "Does anybody know what happened?"

I realised that the police would not have been talkative about the letter-bomb. "Goodness only knows," I said. "Bottle-gas must have escaped somehow from the kitchen—

it's heavier than air, you know, so a slow leak would have left gas low in the room and I wouldn't have noticed it. But I can only guess; the firemen took away the cylinder, so whether it was screwed on properly I'll never know. I'm lucky it was no worse. But I was badly knocked about, and the hospital doctor says that I've got to take things quietly for the next month or so. I'm going to stay with a cousin near Bristol. It would be nice to have the cottage liveable-in to come back to. I wonder if you could help to find a builder who could put in new windows and make the place shipshape?"

"My daughter works in a builder's office in Kingsbridge," she said. "I'm sure she can arrange for something to be done. I'll ask her when she comes home."

"That would be marvellous. Let me give you a cheque for the builder."

She wouldn't have this. "Lord, Mr Blair, we knew your father," she said. "Let the builder do the job, and you can pay when you come back. He won't be worrying."

I thanked her and went back to George. I told him what I'd said about bottle-gas. "Couldn't be better," he said. "We've naturally said nothing about a letter-bomb. A reporter from the local paper got on to Manning, but all he said was that there'd been a domestic explosion and a fire—good police phrases! People laugh at them sometimes, but they've got their uses. If it gets round that there was a leak of bottle-gas people won't ask questions."

George and his wife Mary, a Plymouth woman who had been a schoolteacher, lived at Topsham, in a pleasant, newish house, not far from the golf course. They had two children, a boy of fourteen, and a girl a couple of years younger. Both went to school in Exeter, and I met them when they came home that evening. We had a late tea or early supper to suit

THE LOCKET 47

the children, and then they went off to do their prep. Meeting this lively, intelligent family, I felt again what a mess I had made of my life. After supper, George said, "You've only just come out of hospital, and Mary thinks you need a bit of looking after. She's put a hot water bottle in your bed, and I suggest that you turn in. Tomorrow I'd like you to come to the office with me for a sort of conference."

The conference consisted of George, Detective-Sergeant Manning from Kingsbridge, and me. I don't know what I'd expected the CID headquarters to be like, but there was nothing particularly intimidating about George's office. It was a big, business-like room, lined with steel filing cabinets, but also containing a couple of rather club-like leather armchairs. George sat at a desk much like the one I'd had at Consolidated Investments. Manning, whose Christian name turned out to be Charles, was as cheerful as before. "Can't keep away from the police, can you, Major Blair?" he said as we shook hands. I felt I owed him an apology, though I couldn't think why. Fortunately I didn't have to say anything, for a girl brought in coffee at just the right moment.

When she'd gone, George said, "I've asked Major Blair to meet us here, Charles, so that we can go over everything, and try to draw up some plan of campaign. It's not easy, because we haven't a clue about whom we're fighting. All we know is that the enemy doesn't use very nice weapons. Tell Major Blair what you've been able to discover about the letter."

"Next to nothing, sir," Manning said. "I got to Rivermouth Cottage about half an hour after the explosion—just after the ambulance had gone off. The fire brigade had dealt with the fire—as a matter of fact it had been put out pretty well by the neighbours before the firemen got there. They were hunting around to try to find out what had caused the explosion. There didn't seem any obvious cause, so they telephoned to ask their Chief Officer to come. I waited for him to arrive, and we went over the place together.

"I doubt if we'd have spotted anything if the Chief Officer hadn't recently been on a course about how to deal with incendiary devices. He noticed a bit of charred foil on the floor, and that put us on to it. We sifted all the debris and found three or four pieces of metal that were later shown to have been part of a miniature detonator. It was a tiny thing—about half the size of one of those small fuses that you get in electric plugs. But I'm getting ahead a bit.

"The Chief Fire Officer and I collected everything that seemed interesting or suspicious, including what was left of letters and envelopes. There wasn't much, and they were all charred. I took the lot to the Fire Service's Forensic Laboratory in Hertfordshire. It's a marvellous place. From our bits and pieces they were able to identify the type of bomb that had been used, and to say which pieces of envelope had been in contact with explosive. The chief scientist there was interested in the bomb. He said it was a sort that had not been used much in Europe, though it had been used in the Middle East. It had been developed, apparently, by some urban guerilla group in South America, and was usually pretty deadly. He thought you were lucky to be alive."

"I think so, too," I said.

"Well, to get back to the envelopes. There were only two bits that mattered, both pieces of a brown envelope. One had a typed 'ir' on it—presumably for Blair in the address—and the other, remarkably, an identifiable bit of postmark, which suggested that it had been posted in London, S.W.1."

"I remember it quite clearly," I said. "It was a brown envelope with a typed address. I didn't look at the postmark. I thought it was a circular. It went off as I opened it."

"It was thundering good work by Charles and the Fire Officer," George said. "Unhappily it doesn't get us very far. We can say, I think definitely, that somebody sent you a bomb in a letter or small packet posted in London S.W.1. That doesn't necessarily mean that he lives in S.W.1.—even if it did, it is precious little to go on."

"I doubt if it's worth bothering with that end of things at present," I said. "What matters is something to do with that girl's body. And that happened here—I mean, off Salcombe. If we could find out *what* I'm supposed to have, or to know, that makes me worth killing, we'd be better placed to discover who wants to kill me. I've been going over it all so much in my mind that I can run back the events of that afternoon almost like a film. Sergeant Manning, you were there when we got back to the cove. The body hadn't been moved—it was exactly as I'd left it. Can you recall *anything* lying beside it?"

"No," Manning said.

"You'll have a list of what she had on—I didn't notice anything but her dress, and that she was wearing stockings."

"I've got the inventory of everything found on the body," George said. He went over to a filing cabinet and brought back a folder. "Green short-sleeved dress," he read out, "brassiere, nylon slip and pants, nylon tights—not stockings, Peter, but you wouldn't have noticed, and it doesn't matter, anyway. Thin chain, broken, of yellow metal, probably nine-carat gold. And that's the lot."

"I can see the chain now," I said. "It's the sort of little chain that women wear, with usually a locket, or a crucifix, hanging from it. There wasn't anything on this chain because it was broken—it had only stayed on her because it was caught in her dress. I can't help feeling that the chain is important, somehow—or probably not the chain itself, but whatever was on the end of it."

George and Sergeant Manning both leaned forward. "Go on," George said.

"You must forgive me if this sounds like a detective story," I continued. "But it *is* a detective story, and I'm the hunted man, so I've naturally thought about it backwards, sideways and round the clock. Suppose you are right about this girl's being Gwen Rosing, and suppose you are right in thinking that she was mixed up in some drug-ring, and that for some reason they wanted to get rid of her. Well, there were no signs of a struggle, so we can assume that she went off without suspecting anything, presumably with someone she knew. I think we can assume that she was put in the sea from a boat —knocked out suddenly, if that blow on the temple happened before death, then given a heroin injection to see that she didn't wake up, then put over the side. It would have been risky to do all this on land; and if she'd been put in from the shore, I don't think she'd have fetched up on those rocks in quite the way she did. Anyway, assume for the moment that she was put in from a boat.

"Now we've got to make another assumption, but it's quite a reasonable one—we must assume that she had with her something, perhaps some piece of paper, which was so valuable, or so incriminating, that she always kept it with her. The killer or killers knew this, and they thought it would be in her handbag. They kept her handbag when they threw her in, so they weren't worried about it. *But suppose it wasn't in a handbag, but in a locket that she wore!* They didn't bother about the locket when they threw her in, but when they couldn't find whatever it was they wanted in her handbag, they remembered that she always wore a locket, and they were very worried indeed. When nothing was said about the locket at the inquest they were even more worried. They think I've got the locket."

"It's an interesting reconstruction," George said. "But as you haven't got the locket I don't see that it gets us anywhere."

"Wait a bit," I went on, "I haven't finished. We know that there was no locket with the body because the chain was broken. But when did the chain break? If it broke when they were pushing her overboard, the chances are that they'd have seen the locket fall into the sea. So let's assume that it didn't break then. Would a metal chain break on a body just floating around in the sea? I don't think so. It is much more likely to have broken when she was thrown against the rocks—she was lying face down when I found her, and the locket part of the chain could easily have scraped on the rocks. Maybe the locket is still there, caught in some crack in the rocks, or in the sand near them. It would sink fairly quickly, particularly if it was a heavy sort of locket—it might not have been carried away."

"It's an idea, sir," Manning said, "at least it's an idea."

"Yes," said George, "but it's pretty far-fetched, and needs a hell of a lot of assumptions." He was silent for quite a long time. Then he went on, "But I must say, Peter, that you have produced a theory, and so far we've absolutely nothing else to go on. It's a long chance, but I think we'll have a look round those rocks."

"They uncover at low water," I said, "though there may be a few shallow pools round the outliers. The body went on the rocks from seaward, so if there is anything to be found, I'd expect it to be on the seaward side. Can you get hold of a tide table? I've got nothing else to do, so I might as well sail round in *Lisa* as soon as there's a low tide in daylight."

"You'll do nothing of the sort," George said. "You're supposed to be staying near Bristol. If there's anyone in Salcombe interested in your movements he'll keep an eye on the estuary, and you'd almost certainly be seen sailing out. But I agree that the cove is best approached by sea. Let's have a look at the tides."

CID headquarters have an excellent reference service. A telephone call from George brought back the girl who had given us coffee with a tide table in a matter of minutes. George looked at the figures. "The ebb begins at Salcombe about five minutes after high water at Plymouth, let's say about six minutes later than Plymouth at your cove," he said. "Tomorrow will do very well. It'll be low water at about 0802, should be comfortably light, but not a time when many people are likely to be about—not that the cove would be crowded in November, anyway." He turned to Manning. "Look, Charles, I don't think we'll go round from Salcombe. Can you get over to Dartmouth and get hold of a good tough fishing boat? We don't want the owner. We'll have a police-only crew—the fewer people who know of our treasure hunt the better. I want a chart." He telephoned again, and the girl brought in a coastal chart. He studied it, and ran a ruler over the distances. "Let's see—about two miles to get out of the Dart into Start Bay, and then about eight miles across the bay to Start Point," he said. "Then about another four miles or so to round Prawle Point to get to the cove. That's fourteen—say fifteen—miles all told. You ought to be able to get a boat that will do seven or eight knots—that means a run of about two hours. Allow a bit for wind and tide, perhaps, against us—if we leave at 0530 we ought to be at the cove for dead low water. Get a boat with some shelter, Charles, and something to make a cup of tea, for it will be a cold trip. Ring me from Dartmouth when you've fixed things up. Peter and I will be on the quay at 0500."

A police car called for us at George's house at 0300. Manning had telephoned during the afternoon to say that he'd chartered a forty-foot fishing boat with a wheelhouse, a cabin, and a good diesel engine. Dartmouth police had offered a constable who was an experienced sailor, and he would look after the boat. Since she might have to anchor some way out, there'd be a rubber dinghy to take us ashore.

George and I had gone to bed directly after supper, but I wasn't able to sleep. George came in with a cup of coffee at 02.30. We saw the lights of the police car as it turned into

THE LOCKET

George's road, and we were outside the house waiting for it when it stopped. "Nice timing," George said to the driver.

"Thank you, sir," he replied.

The journey to Dartmouth took about an hour and a half. George, more used than I was to broken nights, dozed most of the way. I was far too excited, and also worried. I was taking up an awful lot of police time. George had been extraordinarily nice, but I couldn't help wondering if he was getting rather fed up with me and my affairs. Suppose—as was more than probable—we found nothing? I should feel wretchedly guilty. Oh, well, at least we were doing *something*, and it was better to be doing anything than sitting still waiting for the next letter-bomb.

We got to the quay nearly half an hour before our estimated time of departure, but Manning was there waiting for us. "The boat's just down the steps," he said. The driver took the car to the police station, and we went on board.

After my yawl, the fishing boat seemed immense. The wheelhouse was workmanlike, but comfortable, raised on a low bridge-deck to give a clear view forward. A companion led down aft into the cabin, and there was a galley below, too, for we'd hardly got on board when the constable who was going to skipper us popped up the companionway with mugs of steaming tea. He was wearing police trousers, but a thick seaman's sweater in place of his tunic. Manning introduced us. Then George glanced at his watch. "We've plenty of time," he said, "but there's no point in staying here. Let's get under way, and lose time, if we need to, on the run across Start Bay."

The constable cast off aft, and then he took the wheel while I went forward to cast off the bow-line. I pushed off with the boathook, and we swung out into the stream.

It was a cold, clear night, with very little wind. I knew the Dart and the entrance to Dartmouth fairly well—it is among the loveliest waterways in the world. A little upstream of where we were was the yard where Chay Blyth's ketch *British Steel* had been built, to take him singlehanded on his fantastic voyage the "wrong way" round the world. I hoped that we might have an equally successful outcome to our adventure.

It was too dark to make out anything of the shore—the shoreline was simply an edge of deeper blackness, with lights, street lamps in the town and an occasional lighted window, here and there. The constable knew what he was doing, and the fishing boat stood purposefully out to sea.

We had to clear the Meg Rocks and round Combe Point to get into Start Bay. The constable kept about a mile offshore, and once properly at sea he laid a course that would take us well clear of the Blackstone rocks off Start Point. When we were on course for our run across the bay he asked me if I would take the wheel for a bit while he got breakfast. I'd not expected such luxury, and when he reappeared with a plate of thick bacon sandwiches I realised that I was hungry. George and Manning had theirs in the cabin. I stayed in the wheelhouse with the constable.

Sunrise was officially at 0736, but there is always more light at sea than there is on land and by the time we cleared Start Point it was possible to make out the coast. I had hoped for a dramatic sunrise, but as it grew near dawn the sky clouded—it was only light cloud, but enough to make the sunrise a haze of dispersed light instead of that glorious burst of colour when the sun suddenly breaks a clear horizon. We rounded Prawle Point and made the cove with a good twenty minutes in hand before dead low water.

We anchored well out, in a couple of fathoms, and the constable and I got the rubber dinghy over the side. "Do you want me to come, sir?" he asked George.

"Might as well," George replied. "The boat will be safe enough in this weather. And four pairs of eyes are better than three."

The dinghy would have taken the four of us, but we were all on the large side, and we reckoned that it would be safer with three. George, Manning and I went first. I took the oars and put George and Manning ashore, and then rowed back for the constable. We hauled the dinghy well up the beach, and walked over to join George and Manning at the rocks.

It seemed hopeless to expect to find anything that had been dropped nearly a month ago. I'd forgotten the seaweed: the rocks were fringed with a thick growth, and it struck me miserably that if a locket had fallen off the girl the weed would have caught and held it for the sea to take—anywhere. However, we'd come to look for a locket, and we'd just have to tackle the job as thoroughly as we could.

We began by making an inspection of the rocks. The landward rocks were the size of a small house, and I didn't see much point in clambering over them, because if anything was to be found it would be on the seaward side, where the girl had been washed up. We could walk right round the rocks now, and I took the party to the flattish rock where the girl's body had been lying. It was steep, the top rising at an angle of about forty degrees from the horizontal, and round the base of the rock on which I'd found the girl was a jagged mass of seaweed-covered broken rock.

"I'm trying to imagine what must have happened," I said. "The tide was making, and the girl floated in with it. Those lower rocks were covered, but of course I don't know precisely how long she'd been there. They may have been not much covered when she was washed over them. The chain may have broken then, before she fetched up on the rock the waves finally put her on."

George nodded. "We'll each take about two yards square," he said, "and probe down as far as we can. Let's try to keep roughly in line, and we'll work our way right round."

Probing that seaweed turned out to be exceedingly difficult

to do. It was tough, leathery stuff, and you had to get down on your knees and force the tangled mass apart with both hands, pulling it away frond by frond. We found plenty of small marine creatures, and the constable cut his hand on a piece of broken bottle, but after half an hour we had nothing to show for our work.

George straightened himself. "The tide's turned," he said, "and it won't be long before these lower rocks are awash. Well, down again, boys. We'll carry on as long as we can."

It was the seaweed that gave us our triumph. I was poking at a little sand-filled crack that I could just get my finger into, when I heard Manning, who was on my left, catch his breath. "I've come across something," he said, "but I don't know what it is, yet." We all stopped our scrabbling and waited while he thrust his whole arm between a mass of seaweed and the rock-face. "Damn," he said. "I can't quite reach. Can somebody hold this stuff apart?"

George went one side of him, I the other. We each pulled an armful of seaweed towards us, while Manning lay down flat and reached as far as he could. "Got it!" he said at last.

George and I held the seaweed apart for him while he carefully withdrew his arm. As his hand came up I saw something glitter. We crowded round him while he looked at it.

"Where exactly did you find it?" I asked.

"It was held in a little crevice, edge-on in the crevice, with seaweed all round it," he said. "It was so jammed in that I had quite a job to get it out. I reckon that the weed held it, and that each incoming tide forced it in a bit. I just noticed something shining when I parted the weed over it."

"A truly marvellous job, Charles," George said.

It was certainly a locket, oval and fairly big, about two and a half inches on its long diameter. It was also quite certainly gold, for when Manning rubbed it on his trousers it shone back, quite untarnished from its contact with seawater.

THE LOCKET

"We won't open it here. Let's get back on board," George said. "God, what a piece of luck!"

Since we wanted now to get off as quickly as we could, I took Manning and the constable on board first, and rowed back for George. As soon as the dinghy was stowed the constable started the engine, and Manning and I got in the anchor. When we were under way, Manning and I joined George in the cabin. He was sitting on the settee-berth, with the locket on his handkerchief in front of him on the cabin table. The locket was a beautiful piece of work, early Victorian, I thought, the gold intricately chased, and the faces fitting together so perfectly that you could scarcely see the line where they joined.

"I wonder how it opens?" George said. There was a little knob on top, like the winder of a watch, holding the ring to attach it to a chain. He pressed the knob, but nothing happened. "No," he said, "it doesn't press." He looked at it closely, and added, "I think, perhaps, it slides." He tried sliding the knob. It was stiff, but after a moment it moved, and the front face of the locket sprang open. Inside was a piece of folded paper. The locket was so beautifully made that it was almost waterproof. The edges of the paper were slightly discoloured, but only the edges. He opened it, and it became a page, five inches by three, from a loose-leaf notebook. There was no writing, but a column of figures:

```
50167309
200013530
182710550
40189611
63327918
51230231
321910728
```

The three of us studied it for a long time. "God alone

knows what it means," George said. "Of course, it may be nothing to do with the girl at all."

"No," I said. "But if you find a girl with a broken locket-chain, and you find a locket where the chain must have broken, it's a reasonable assumption that they belong together."

Nobody disputed this, but it didn't seem all that helpful.

We lunched in Dartmouth, a noble meal which George insisted on standing us, and for which we were all ready. He told the constable, "I don't think you need to make any report on this. In fact, I'd rather you didn't—the less people know about our treasure hunt the better. I'll call at the station before we leave, and explain things. You did very well, indeed, and I'll see that a note goes in about it."

The constable was suitably grateful.

We drove back via Kingsbridge, to drop Manning. When the three of us were in the car I couldn't help noticing a slightly new feeling of respect for me.

"I just don't know how you thought it out, Peter," George said. "Charles and I are trained detectives, and we didn't."

"Sergeant Manning found the locket," I said.

"Maybe. But neither he nor I thought of looking for it."

"You weren't thinking for your lives," I said.

Manning asked if he could have a copy of the figures on the piece of paper. George read them out, and Manning wrote them down in his notebook. "Wet towels ahead," said George.

We dropped Manning at Kingsbridge police station, and for the first few miles towards Totnes George was silent. Then he said, "What on earth do you make of it, Peter?"

"Nothing so far," I replied. "When you were reading out the figures you paused a little after the first couple of pairs. You made them sound a bit like latitudes and longitudes."

"Good Lord," he said. "I wonder! We'll go straight to the office and have a look at the chart."

"I fancy you'll need an atlas rather than a chart," I said. "Still, it may be just worth having a look."

George put the paper from the locket on his desk, and we both studied it. "If the figures are navigational," I said, "there are four possibilities for each group, reading across. The first lot could be latitude either north or south, the next longitude east or west. I think we can rule out latitudes south of the equator, at least for the moment. Let's see—50 16 73 09." I turned to a map of the world in the atlas. "That puts us roughly in the Hudson Strait if it's west longitude, about the middle of Siberia if it's east. Not very encouraging, but we'll try the next lot—20 00 135 30. Mid-Pacific, west, between the Philippines and the Marianas, east. No, George, it's not worth going on with this."

"They're funny figures, all the same," he said. "Suppose they *are* positions, but in code."

I considered this. "Nothing to show one way or the other," I said. "As straightforward geographical positions, the figures don't seem to make sense. In code—well, unless we can break the code we don't know what they may mean."

George sat back in his chair. "Listen," he said. "I told you that I thought this girl Gwen Rosing was mixed up in a drug-ring. I've no real evidence for this, but everything that's happened since you found her fits in with the idea that there's some very nasty work going on. Those figures must mean something—and they must mean something desperately important to somebody, or you wouldn't have come in for all this attention on the mere chance that you might have them.

"I've told you that we don't know how this heroin is coming into the country. Yes, of course, there are half-a-hundred routes—aircraft crews, seamen, tourists bringing cars back from the Continent, all sorts of possible ways. But we're not exactly idle, you know. And police and Customs between us, we've a lot of experience of all these things. There have been the usual little hauls, but nothing in the past year or so big enough to account for the quantities of heroin now being distributed. What's more, everything points to some *regularity* of supply—some source, that is, that the distributors can rely on, instead of chancing on all these various other people, who may or may not get through.

"Now, Peter, you're a dinghy sailor. My boy is keen on sailing, too, and we went this year to Salcombe Regatta. I'd never really thought about dinghies much before, but when I saw those fleets of small boats all together, it struck me that there must be thousands and thousands of them round every estuary in Britain. And who bothers when a dinghy goes out or comes in? Could this damnable heroin be coming in by dinghy? Come into the map-room for a moment."

We went about two doors down the corridor from George's office to a room with its walls covered with maps. Most of them were road-maps of various parts of Devon and Cornwall, but there was a good big map of the British Isles. George stood in front of it.

"Most of the coast can be ruled out, I think," he said. "Remember, I'm talking about dinghies. Scotland and all the East Coast north of the Wash is too far from the Continent. The West Coast and the Bristol Channel has access to Ireland, but it's a bit far, and the Irish Sea is not dinghy-sailing water. God knows there's been trouble enough in Ireland, but there's nothing to suggest an Irish depot for the drug traffic. The South Coast, from Dover to Eastbourne, is the best bet for a quick nip across the Channel, but it's also the most populous coast, and the Customs there have centuries of experience in looking out for small-boat smugglers. Move on to our part of the world. From Exmouth to Plymouth and on to Looe and Fowey you have a broken coast with myriads of little coves, and you have dozens of sailing centres where dinghies are so familiar that no one takes the least notice of them. If there's anything in my dinghy theory, this would seem to be the coast to operate from. But could it be done? Could your yawl, say, safely go across to France?"

"How long is a piece of string?" I answered. "A thirteen-foot boat has crossed the Atlantic. A sixteen-foot dinghy could certainly sail from the Devon coast to France. I've done it myself—I've been across to Carteret in *Lisa*. But it's a long trip. It took me nearly forty hours, and you have to watch the weather. Given a spell of settled weather, fair enough, but I wouldn't undertake now to sail to France next week. And what's even less easy from your point of view is making a French port. You say nobody notices dinghies—well, it's not quite true. You don't notice your *own* dinghies, but anyone with half an eye for a boat notices strangers. The French are nice to small boats, but they're pretty strict, all the same. I had to report to the police, show my passport, fill in various forms. I suppose I could have picked up a suitcase of heroin, but I don't see it as a regular trade. It wouldn't be long before somebody started getting interested in an English dinghy that kept on popping in and out.

"But—wait a minute, George. Why bother to go over to France? You could meet a boat four or five miles off shore, pick up your parcel and go back, all in three or four hours. You wouldn't be away mysteriously—you'd go out for the day, or the afternoon, and come back, as people are doing all the time. Yes, George, it could be done."

"And those figures could be the rendezvous, perhaps?"

"Well, if we knew what they meant."

We went back to George's office. He put the locket and the original piece of paper in a safe, but we both made copies of it before it was locked away. "Let's go home," he said. "We've had a long day. Mary will be out—she's gone with the kids to a school play. But she'll have left some supper for us, and after we've had a drink and something to eat maybe you'll have some more brilliant ideas."

I didn't feel brilliant. I wasn't even hungry after our excellent lunch at Dartmouth, but I was ready for George's whisky. Mary Payne had left us enough food for a regiment. We made little impression on it, and after we'd done our best I helped George to wash up. "I don't usually drink after supper," he said, "but tonight I think we could both do with some more whisky. Come into the den."

The "den" was his study, furnished in much the same style as his office but smaller, and with chairs upholstered in a dark blue cloth instead of leather. He poured me a generous whisky and we sat down.

"If that thing is a code," he said, "why is it so valuable? Why don't they change it?"

I'd been thinking of this, too, and with a rather more directly personal concern than George. "There could be any number of reasons," I said. "We don't know anything about the organisation. If it's scattered, with agents in various parts of the world it may take a long time to get in touch with everybody, or they may not want to risk meetings. And they might not like sending codes by post. We haven't many facts, but we have got a few—one of them being the attempt to kill me. One would think that it would be much easier to make a new code than to go to all the trouble of murder. We don't know why the figures are so important to them, but I think we can say that they still are important."

"And we may never discover what they mean," George said.

"True enough. That's another gamble they could take. They don't *know* that anybody has the locket—until today we hadn't. They may *think* I have it, and that therefore I'm safer out of the way, but they don't *know*. They may reckon that if I'm dead, or sufficiently frightened, the code itself is safe enough—as a code, I mean." George shrugged his shoulders, and I changed the subject.

"Let's get back to thinking about the girl," I said. "There's a fearful lot about her that absolutely fogs me. You say that she was really Gwen Rosing, and you think that she was deliberately put in the sea. If so, all that business about the hotel booking was a fake. And why the elaborate arrangements about the letter in the suitcase? If they wanted to get rid of her, why not just get rid of her and hope that she would never be found? Why draw attention to her disappearing in such a dramatic way?"

"Somebody wanted her dead as Edna Brown," George said. "It wasn't enough for her to disappear—Edna Brown had to be shown to be dead. They couldn't count on her body being washed up, but the letter took care of that. It didn't need a body. Miss Brown said plainly that she was going to drown herself, and whether or not her body was discovered there wouldn't be much doubt that she was dead. You see, Miss Brown existed all right—she worked for that advertising agency, and she lived in her flat. She wasn't reported missing, because she was supposed to be on holiday —all that was perfectly genuine. But when she didn't come back from her holiday, somebody, either her flat-mate or her office, would almost certainly have started making inquiries. In any case, when she didn't turn up at the hotel, the manager would naturally be concerned about his bill, and also what to do about the suitcase. He'd either have opened the case himself, or brought it to us. Then the letter would have come to light, and of course we'd make inquiries about Miss Brown. She'd be listed as missing, and if no more was heard of her we'd assume—in view of the letter—that she had done what she said she was going to do, and that she was dead. If whoever killed her wanted the police to know that Edna Brown was dead, he acted very cleverly."

"Do you know how he managed the letters—the letters to the hotel?"

"Well, when the letter came to light we had a dead girl on our hands, and, as you know, the post mortem had made us particularly interested in her. So we made very detailed inquiries. The Metropolitan Police are as much concerned as we are. I interviewed Miss Wilberforce at the flat, and I also saw Mr Potterton at the agency. The Metropolitan Police made a lot of discreet inquiries among the staff of the agency. Everything seemed above board—at least in the life of the girl called Edna Brown. She was quite often away for two or three days, but that was explained by her work for the agency. The set-up is as much Public Relations as advertising and it seems a flourishing concern, with clients all over the place. They arrange local Press conferences for various people, usually with a fairly lavish cocktail party thrown in. One of Miss Brown's jobs was to organise these parties, and by all accounts she did it very well."

"If you are right, she was not exactly inexperienced," I said.

"Perhaps not. But these were eminently respectable parties. They were meant for publicity."

"You haven't told me about the letters. I'm still puzzled about that."

"What about the letters?"

"The letters to and from the hotel. If Miss Brown was done away with, presumably she didn't write them herself."

"Well, it wouldn't have been difficult. The address given was her flat, and anybody can type any address. The hotel replied to the flat, and that may have been a bit more tricky. But it isn't really a flat—it's the bottom half of one of those big Victorian London houses. It's let as a flat to Miss Wilberforce, but four other girls live there. Each has a room, and what was once the drawing room of the house is a sort of communal sitting room. A caretaker lives in the basement.

He's an elderly man, and I don't think he does much. His wife does a bit of cleaning for the girls, and there's a similar sort of typists' collective or whatever you like to call it in the top half of the house. The caretaker or his wife collects letters, and puts them on a table in the hall. The girls look through the post and help themselves. They are all coming and going at different times, so it's a pretty loose arrangement. Most of the girls have boy friends, and they are always coming and going, too—though Miss Brown, it seems, seldom had visitors at the flat. Anyone capable of the kind of planning we've envisaged wouldn't have had much trouble in getting hold of a couple of letters addressed to Miss Brown."

George stretched his arms. "Lord, I'm tired," he said. "And I've decided what to do next. I'm going up to London tomorrow to discuss our treasure hunt with the chaps I've been working with in London. You can come too, if you like —you're a material witness, and I daresay they'd like to interview you."

4
Fifth Girl

WE DIDN'T GO to the new police building near Victoria that has replaced the famous Scotland Yard, but to a room at the Home Office in Whitehall. George had explained on the train. "It's a newish set-up," he said, "and I think a good one. You know, we suffer from our history—the police as much as any other British institution. In a rather vague way all police forces come under the Home Office, but only the Metropolitan Police are controlled directly by the Home Secretary. The rest of us come under a variety of County Council watch committees. A number of the smaller forces have been grouped together over the past few years, but control is still supposed to be local. I know that this is believed to be a great safeguard of democracy, in that there is no national police boss who can give orders to every policeman, but I doubt if there's much in it. The system worked well enough when crime was largely local, but in these days of the highly mobile criminal it has disadvantages. It's not that there's any lack of co-operation between us—there's a good network of communication, and we all know that we're trying to do the same job. The old idea that I get frustrated and indignant if a London officer trespasses on my manor is certainly no longer true, if it ever was. Most of us are so damned busy that we are only too thankful if we can hand over an awkward case to someone else. No, the real lack is that we haven't really got anything in the way of a Police General Staff. It's like leaving Divisional Commanders to fight a war without an Army Staff to direct strategy. We try to get over it by having all sorts of liaison committees. The one we're going to is an experiment in that it works quite informally—which is why I can take you with me. It was set up primarily to plan strategy in the campaign against drugs, though it may take on other jobs later. The head isn't even a policeman—he's a Deputy Secretary at the Home Office called Edmund Pusey. He's a good man, and very intelligent. He's got a small permanent staff, and direct access to the CID, the Special Branch and everybody else who matters. I'm not sure who'll be there this afternoon. I told him we were coming, and, of course, he knows what it's all about."

I took to Pusey at once. He got up to meet us, and couldn't have been more friendly. "It is good of you to come, Major Blair," he said as I was introduced. He indicated the others, "Commander Paul Seddon, of the CID, and Inspector Rodney Charrington, of the Special Branch." We all shook hands. "Now what have you got for us, George?" he asked.

George produced the locket, which we'd collected from his safe on the way to the station at Exeter. Pusey studied the gold chasing intently. "Have you noticed the monogram?" he said.

"To tell the truth," said George, "I haven't really examined the locket. We only found it yesterday, and we were all more concerned with the paper inside it."

"Well, have a look," said Pusey. "It's involved, but beautifully done, and quite clear when you've worked it out. L.C.—now, isn't that interesting?"

He passed round the locket, and we all had a look. The intricate engraving gave a first impression of being merely a design of loops and whirls, but when you looked into it you could see that it embodied the letters L.C. I was annoyed that we'd missed it. But George was right—we'd rather dismissed the locket as the container of what it held.

"Why is L.C. specially interesting?" Inspector Charrington asked.

"Because Gwen Rosing's maternal great-grandmother was Lady Luella Carstairs," Pusey said. "She was the wife of the third Earl, I believe, and by all accounts was as hot a little thing as her great-granddaughter. It's another indication, George, that your dead girl was La Rosing."

"I wonder if that's really why they're after me," I said.

Pusey considered. "Maybe, but it's a bit far-fetched," he said. "You'd have to know the name of one of Gwen Rosing's great-grandmothers, and I doubt if that could be expected of you. I doubt if they knew it themselves. I only knew it because I've been into her history." He paused, and went on, "It's an interesting, and sad, history. All that was known of her when she filled the papers was that she'd run away from an orphanage in Manchester and lived by her wits—if that's the way to put it—in London until she got a job in a strip-tease show. There she was taken up by Rupert Hare, the property man, and the rest followed. Actually, she came of what would be called a good family, though they'd completely disowned her. Her father—at least, the husband of her mother—was the Hon. Jeremy Maylock. He divorced his wife soon after Gwen was born and went off to live in Rhodesia, where he died. The mother was mixed up with various other men, keeping Gwen with her, which is a good mark, because it can't have been all that easy for her. Finally, she went to live with a man called Rosing, and they were killed together in a car crash one night when they were both pretty drunk. Gwen was about six. There was no money, and apparently no relations, so she was taken into care by the local authority and put in the orphanage. Odd that she managed to keep the locket. She must have loved it very much."

"And moving that she should have been wearing it when she died," I said.

"Yes." Pusey tapped his desk. "But we mustn't get sentimental about her. One can pity—but she helped to wreck a lot of other people's lives. After the storm broke—before she disappeared—she tried to backmail her Maylock relations, but they came straight to us, and she was warned off. If she turned to drug-pushing it was even worse. I wish we knew a bit more about Edna Brown. The advertising agency appears to have been her first job, and she got an employment card when she joined. Before that—nothing. She doesn't even seem to have been born. She put a date and place of birth on her form when she had to clock in for National Insurance, but it's been impossible to confirm them."

I had an idea, but said nothing for the moment. Pusey picked up the locket again. "How does it open, George?" he asked.

George slid back the knob, and took out the folded paper. Pusey looked at it, and passed it to Commander Seddon. "You're a bit of an expert on codes," he said. "What do you make of it?"

Seddon studied the figures intently. "It looks more like a key than a message," he said. "The groups aren't regular, though—four of them have eight digits, three have nine. If it is the key to a code, I'd say it was a code for enciphering numbers rather than words or letters. There are fifty-nine digits in all, which doesn't fit any alphabet. And there are not nearly enough groups for a word-book."

"Major Blair suggested that they might be latitudes and longitudes," George said.

"That was only because of the way you read them out," I put in.

"They could be," Seddon said. "Each line could be a position in degrees, minutes, and seconds, but you'd have to guess north or south, east or west."

"But they don't make sense," I said. "We looked up some

of them, and they're all over the place, from the Arctic to the Pacific."

"All the same, I wish they were," George said.

"You can't do much with a code if you haven't got a message," Seddon observed. "We've come across nothing so far in the way of coded messages."

"Perhaps because we haven't looked for them," Pusey said. "If there is a code, what would it have to do?"

"Enable a group of perhaps scattered people to exchange information," I suggested.

"Yes. And how would they communicate? By post—telegrams—telephone?"

Charrington cut in. "Could be anything," he said, "but I'd rule out the telephone. Figures aren't reliable in telephonic codes—it's too easy to mishear a figure."

"I think we can narrow it a bit more," Pusey said. "The people we're dealing with don't want anyone to know that they are even in touch with one another. Charrington's right about the telephone. Letters and telegrams have the disadvantage that they must be sent to an address. This doesn't look like a code for elaborate messages—there's not enough of it. How about short messages in the personal column of a newspaper? They could convey a warning, news of the arrival of a consignment, things like that."

"Well, that's something we *can* look for," Seddon said. "Nothing may come of it, but at least we can try. We can go through the files for the past couple of years and see if there are any numeral-messages in the personal columns that could conceivably fit these groups. It'll take a bit of time, but I'll get someone on to it tomorrow."

We talked of my adventures for a bit, until George said that he had to get back to Exeter, and we must leave for Paddington.

"If you don't mind, George," I said, "I think I'll stay in

London for a few days. I want to call on Miss Wilberforce. I don't know whether you noticed at the inquest, but she rather implied that while Miss Brown was always going out, she herself didn't get so many invitations. She looked a pleasant enough young woman, but she wasn't exactly sparkling. I thought I'd try inviting her to dinner. I can do it quite reasonably—I can say that finding myself in London I felt I'd like to pay my respects to her, seeing that we were both mixed up in such a sad business." The CID man seemed about to say something, so I went on hurriedly. "Please—I know I'm not a policeman, but I'm as much involved in this affair as anyone, and you'll admit that I've the strongest reasons for trying to get it cleared up. The very fact that I'm not a policeman may just possibly let Miss Wilberforce say something, or remember something, that might be useful."

"I don't like it," George said. "I'm still very much concerned about your safety."

Pusey came to the rescue. "I think Major Blair has a point," he said. "We can't stop him calling on Miss Wilberforce if he wants to—and why should we? As he says, it's just possible that the girl may tell him something. I do agree that he may be in some personal danger. I'm going to ask him to let us know where he is staying, and to let us know of all his movements. You get back to Exeter, George, and we'll look after Major Blair."

"I still don't like it," said George, "but you're the boss. Well, goodbye, Peter, and good luck."

"Give my respects to Mary, please, and all my thanks," I said to him. "I'll try to thank you properly later. I'll come back to your house if I may."

"Of course," he said.

Pusey had a flat in Carlton House Terrace, and he asked if I'd stay to dinner. I said I'd love to, but could I first go out and buy some pyjamas and a toothbrush, and find myself a hotel? He said that he'd see to the hotel while I shopped, and suggested that I came back to the flat. I just had time to do my shopping in Victoria Street before the shops shut. It's surprising how much one needs when one has no home base. I bought pyjamas, handkerchiefs, socks, a couple of shirts, toothbrush, razor, and the rest, and a suitcase to put them in. I went to dinner feeling much better equipped, and spent a most pleasant evening with Pusey and his wife.

I didn't enjoy being back in London—there were too many memories. It didn't seem much use calling on Miss Bunty Wilberforce before about six o'clock, so I had the day on my hands. I went to a branch of my bank and arranged to draw some money, and then I thought I'd try a cinema. But there seemed nothing on but horror films, so I went to the British Museum instead, dutifully ringing a number that Pusey had given me to say that I was doing so. I bought some books in Great Russell Street and went back to the hotel for lunch and the rest of the afternoon and was thankful when the time came to set off for Earl's Court.

George's description of what he'd called the typists' collective had prepared me for the house. A girl opened the door, and I asked for Miss Wilberforce. "Yes, I think she's in," she said. "Along the passage, second door on the right." She went off and left me.

There was a card on the door saying "Bunty Wilberforce" so it seemed to be all right. I knocked, and a voice called out, "Who's there?"

"Peter Blair," I said, though I doubted if it could mean anything to her. However, the voice called back in quite a friendly fashion, "Half a minute. I must put something on."

I must have waited at least two minutes, when the door opened and Miss Wilberforce appeared. "I've just got back from the office, and I had to change," she said. "What is it?"

"We've not exactly met, but we have seen each other," I said. "May I come in for a moment?"

She looked puzzled, but let me in. "I have seen you before," she said, "but where?"

I explained, and added that if by any chance she was free I should be most honoured if she'd let me take her out to dinner. She was frankly pleased. "Well, that's very nice of you," she said. "No, I'm not doing anything much. Where shall we go?"

My years with Sybil had at least been an education in restaurants. I suggested a small place in Jermyn Street. She'd obviously heard of it, and was equally obviously impressed. "Good Lord," she said, "if we're going there I shall have to change again. Do you mind waiting in the hall?"

I asked if there was a telephone, so that I could get a taxi while she changed. "Yes," she said. "You'll find a telephone in the hall, and there's a list of taxi numbers beside it. I won't be long."

The telephone was one of those hooded things and it had a coin box. By some miracle there was actually a taxi on the rank, and the driver agreed to come. He was at the door before Miss Wilberforce reappeared, but he said that he would wait a few minutes. She emerged before he got restive, and we drove off.

The restaurant was a good choice, for most of its trade is fairly late, and at that time of evening it was all but empty. The head waiter offered us a nice, secluded table, which I accepted, but said that we'd have a drink at the small bar first. Miss Wilberforce said that she'd have a Martini, so I ordered a large one, and a large whisky for myself. She giggled slightly. "Ooh, I'm not very used to this, you know." But she was clearly ready to enjoy herself.

"The inquest must have been an ordeal for you," I said. "I thought you did wonderfully."

"It was all horrible," she replied, "particularly having to

look at her body. And really, I scarcely knew her. But I had to go because the flat's in my name, so she was a sort of tenant of mine, though actually it's a sharing arrangement."

"How do you manage it?" I asked.

"Well, it's a common thing nowadays. Any sort of flat is so expensive that most girls can only get a place by clubbing together. I went there first with two other girls, but we decided that we'd have to get two more, because the rent was too much for three of us. With five, we pay £8 a week, which isn't too bad. And the owner does jolly well. He gets £35 a week—and for only half the house—but we pay £8 to include a bit for cleaning, and to keep up a small fund for breakages and things. The only trouble is that girls are leaving all the time—to get married, because they change their jobs, for all sorts of reasons, often pretty silly ones, or that's what I think. I'm the only one left of our original lot. But I'm in charge of the typing pool for Brown and Cantilade, the big City solicitors, and I shan't give up that job in a hurry."

"How do you get a new girl when one goes?"

"Oh, it's not too difficult. I put an advertisement in the paper—you must have seen the sort of thing—'Fifth girl wanted, own room, Earl's Court'. That usually brings two or three replies."

"Where was Edna Brown before? Where did she write from?"

"They hardly ever write. She telephoned, like they all do. I suppose I ought to ask for references, but I don't bother as a rule, unless there's something I don't like about a girl. If I do ask for references, mostly they don't come back. I don't think it's because they're not respectable, or anything like that. It's just too much trouble. They ring up, they come along in the evening, and sometimes they move in next day. I try to get a month's rent in advance, but if a girl seems all right, I'll accept two weeks. Mostly they're all right about paying, but I've had to chase some of them for the rent. I'll say this for Edna, though, there was never any trouble with her. She paid a month's rent when she came, and she went on paying, always a month in advance."

The waiter was hovering round us with two enormous menu-cards. "Ooh, how lovely," Miss Wilberforce said. She chose smoked salmon and Boeuf Stroganov. I joined her with the salmon, but followed with a lamb cutlet. The waiter went off with the orders, and I got her another Martini.

There was no problem in getting her to talk—my difficulty was to get a word in edgeways. She regaled me over dinner with long descriptions of all the other women in the typing pool, and reflections on the virtue of most of them. I learned that there was no Mr Brown left in the firm, but two Mr Cantilades, father and son. Old Mr Cantilade was a dear, but the son thought too much of himself, and you had to watch him.

When the sweet-trolley came round I contrived to get back to Miss Brown.

"What did she do with herself at weekends?" I asked.

Between mouthfuls of an exceptionally large chocolate éclair, she replied, "Well, I wouldn't know. She was hardly ever there. She kept herself to herself—we all do, rather, though sometimes a couple of girls may work in the same office, or be friends. Edna was away a lot. She explained when she came that her job often took her out of London— she arranged meetings and things for clients of her firm. She certainly had boy friends, but they didn't often come for her. They used to phone, and I suppose she would go off and meet them somewhere. The three of us on the ground floor get the worst of the phone—and the front door—because one or other of us usually has to answer it. Edna was better off there—she had a room on the next floor. If she was wanted on the phone I'd see if she was in, and if she wasn't I'd leave a note on the hall table—there's a pad there for phone messages. I can't remember ever taking a long message for her, though. It was always would she ring Bill, or Joe, or whoever. I don't remember any of them ever giving a number. Sometimes I'd ask if there was a number—I'd been trained to do that when I worked on a switchboard—but they'd just say 'Oh, she'll know', and ring off."

"Were you surprised that she was going to have a baby?"

"Very surprised. Oh, I know that a lot of girls sleep around nowadays, and I daresay she did, but—but—it's hard to say—she was such a cool, finished person. If she'd wanted a baby, I'd have thought she'd have had one. She wasn't at all the sort of person to go off like that and kill herself." Miss Wilberforce heaved a great sigh. "Just shows how you never know. Takes all sorts, doesn't it?" she said. I ordered her a crème de menthe.

In the taxi going back to Earl's Court, she said, "Well, Mr Blair, it's been ever so nice. Funny, I did recognise you when you came in, but I just couldn't place you at once. Do you remember that other man at the inquest—Mr Potterton, the man from the agency? I'm sure I've seen him before, somewhere, but for the life of me I can't remember where."

Having gone out to dinner early, it was still respectably early when we got back—not quite ten o'clock. I paid the taxi and said I'd enjoy the walk to Earl's Court tube station. Miss Wilberforce hesitated on the doorstep. "You've given me a lovely evening, Mr Blair," she said. "I've got a kettle in my room. Won't you come in for a moment and have a cup of coffee?"

Feeling a little nervous, I accepted.

I needn't have been nervous. Miss Wilberforce was essentially a homely soul and it seemed sad that she wasn't making some suburban commuter a good wife. Perhaps she would. She fussed over the kettle and the coffee pot, chattering away about the smallness of the world, and how you never knew when you got up in the morning what was going to happen. I felt that her real problem was that she knew only too well what was going to happen to her days, and that she was both bored and lonely.

She poured the coffee, and she was beginning to ask whether I could have a meal with her next week, when we heard the front doorbell ring. She took no notice, but it went on ringing. "Oh dear," she said, "that means I've got to answer it. There's probably no one else in."

She was away for two or three minutes, and came back looking bothered. "There's a young man at the door asking for a girl I've never heard of," she said. "I've told him no one of that name lives here, but he won't go away."

"Better find out what it's all about," I said. "I'll protect you."

She gave a little laugh and went off again, returning with a worried-looking youngster, approaching his middle twenties. "I'm Simon Kirby," he said, "and I badly want to see Sheila Mortimer."

"There isn't any Sheila Mortimer here, and never has been, as far as I know," said Miss Wilberforce.

"But I *know* this is the right address," the young man insisted. "She wrote it down for me herself. She told me never to come here unless it was in an emergency. But I do feel this is an emergency, so I *had* to come."

"Could it be one of the girls in the other part of the house?" I asked Miss Wilberforce.

"No," she replied firmly. "They have a separate doorbell, but they have to use our letter-box, so I know their names because of sorting out letters. Theirs go on the other end of the hall table. There isn't anyone called Mortimer."

"I've got a photograph of her," said the young man. He took a coloured snapshot from his wallet and handed it to

Miss Wilberforce. She looked at it, and gasped, "It's—it's Edna!"

I took the snapshot from her. It showed a pretty, fair-haired girl sitting on a garden roller. I'd seen Edna Brown only in death, with her face horribly scarred. This was a girl smiling happily. Perhaps there was a look of Edna Brown about her; beyond that I couldn't say. But Miss Wilberforce had known her. "I'm sure it's Edna," she said.

"I think you'd better sit down," I said to the young man. "Bunty, may I give him a cup of coffee?" I'd not called her Bunty before and I'm not sure whether she noticed it, but it slightly eased the tension. She nodded, and sat down herself, while I poured out coffee.

"There may be some mistake, Mr Kirby," I said, "but if your friend was the girl who lived here as Edna Brown, you must prepare yourself for a shock. Edna Brown is dead."

"Sheila can't be dead," said Kirby. "We were engaged to be married."

"I'm afraid death doesn't always respect engagements," I said as gently as I could. "Tell us about your Sheila, and we'll see if we can help."

He'd met her in Cambridge, he said, where he was doing post-graduate work in geology at St James's College. That would be five or six months ago. She lived in London and had a job that meant a fair bit of travelling. It brought her to Cambridge quite often, and they started going out together. Then she took to coming to Cambridge most weekends, not to work but just to meet him. They planned to be married early in the New Year. He had a reasonable chance of a Fellowship next year. They had started looking for a house. They'd last met just over a month ago. She had been a little strange, and told him that he couldn't see her for a couple of weeks because there was something she had to do, which meant going to another part of England. She wouldn't tell him what it was, but said she'd get in touch with him as soon as she got back.

When he hadn't heard from her after three weeks, he began to be worried. When a month went by he was very worried indeed.

They used to write to each other before she went away, but she had told him not to write to this address. He'd sent letters to her to be collected from a newsagent's shop which she said she passed on her way to work. She'd never been very explicit, but he understood that she lived at Earl's Court with her people, who rather wanted her to marry someone else. That was why she'd told him not to come there.

Now he had to do something. He'd been to the newsagent's shop, but they didn't know anything about her, except that she paid 50p a week to use the address: it was apparently part of their business to offer an accommodation address. She had called once or twice a week to collect letters, but there hadn't been many for her. "Only mine, I suppose," he remarked. But she hadn't been there for some weeks. "There'll be some letters from me waiting for her," he added, "but they wouldn't show them to me. Fair enough, because they didn't know me," he added.

The only thing left seemed to be to come to this house. He'd hung around on several evenings hoping to see her come out. Tonight he felt so desperate that he'd come to the door and rung the bell.

It was an awkward situation. There were a lot of things I wanted to ask Simon Kirby, but I didn't want to be tied to Miss Wilberforce while I asked. I looked at my watch. "Bunty, it's getting late," I said. "I shall have to go. I think Mr Kirby had better come with me. We can walk to Earl's Court station together, and I can tell him about Miss Brown on the way. There's obviously been some crazy mistake, but it's not really anything to do with us. When am I going to see you again?" She brightened up at this, but it turned out not to be so easy. I said I had to go back to Devon in the morning, but that I'd be coming to London again, though I wasn't quite sure when. I promised to let her know. And perhaps one day she could pay a visit to Frogmore. It wasn't very satisfactory because she wanted to go on talking, but I was firm and made my escape, taking Kirby with me.

"Where are you staying?" I asked him.

"I've got friends who live near Victoria, and they've given me a bed for tonight," he said. "Tomorrow I have to be back in Cambridge."

I had a sudden thought. "There's a great deal that ought to be explained to you," I said, "but we can't talk in the street. And it's near closing time, so the pubs will be horrible. Will you come in a taxi with me to the house of a friend of mine? We could talk there."

He was so unhappy that he was ready to do anything. We got a taxi near Earl's Court station, and I gave the address of Pusey's flat in Carlton House Terrace.

I was worried that Pusey might be out, or have gone to bed, but he opened the door himself, and seemed quite unsurprised at our late call. "Come in and have a drink," he said.

He took us into his study, and I introduced Simon Kirby. To Kirby I said, "Mr Pusey is a senior Government official. He is absolutely to be trusted. If you will let me tell him what you told me, it is possible that he can help to solve your problem, though you may not like what you hear."

Kirby just nodded. I repeated his story to Pusey, who asked if we might see his photograph. He produced it again, saying, "I took it myself, in one of the College gardens."

Pusey looked at it carefully. "Yes," he said. "I would say that this is Edna Brown. Does Mr Kirby know what happened to her?"

"I've told him that Edna Brown is dead," I said. "But I have not yet told him of the circumstances."

Pusey took over from me. "I fear that this will be exceedingly distressing," he said. "But one must try to take life's blows without flinching." He gave a straight concise account of my finding of a girl's body on the rocks, of the autopsy showing that she was some three months pregnant, of the letter by which she was identified, and of the findings at the inquest.

Kirby listened in absolute silence. Then he said, "Do you have the letter?"

"No," said Pusey "but I have a copy of it." He opened a drawer of his desk and took out a folder. It held a sheaf of typed papers, one of which was a copy of Edna Brown's letter. He read it aloud, then handed it to Kirby.

"There's no doubt that she was pregnant?" Kirby asked.

"There can be no doubt, I think. The medical evidence was precise," Pusey replied.

Kirby said nothing more for several minutes. Then he got up suddenly. "I don't believe a word of it," he said.

Pusey took a decision. "Neither do I," he observed quietly.

"Just who are you?" Kirby asked. He was beginning to get angry.

"Major Blair's part in things has been explained," Pusey replied calmly. "I work at the Home Office, in a department concerned with such things as inquests. There are many puzzling features of this case, Mr Kirby, and I may say that police inquiries are far from closed. You cannot bring Edna Brown back to life. You may be of service to her memory."

Kirby ran his hand through his hair, but he sat down again. He was not angry now, just miserably unhappy.

"But my fiancée is Sheila Mortimer, not Edna Brown," he said.

"Miss Mortimer lived at the address of the girl known

there as Edna Brown. Miss Mortimer disappeared at about the time that Edna Brown disappeared. Miss Wilberforce, who identified Edna Brown at the inquest, has identified your Miss Mortimer with Edna Brown. Why there are two names involved, we do not yet know—it is not necessarily blameworthy for a woman to be known by different names in different branches of her life. She may have good reasons for it. But the evidence suggests strongly that the girl you knew as Sheila Mortimer died as Edna Brown." Pusey's summing up was convincing.

Kirby seemed beginning to be convinced. "There was always something a bit mysterious about her," he said. "She would never tell me much about herself—who her people were, where she lived as a kid, for instance. I took her to meet my parents at Canterbury—my father is a Canon of the cathedral there—and they liked her very much. I wanted to meet her parents, but she always put me off. As I said, I had the impression that they wouldn't have wanted her to marry me. It was only an impression, though. She never actually said so. But she was very firm about not wanting me to call at Earl's Court."

"May I ask you a very personal question?" Pusey said.

"Go ahead."

"Would it have been possible for you to be the father of her unborn child?"

"Yes," Kirby said simply. "But that's the really damnable part about it," he went on. "Sheila and I spent several weekends together. She loved the Cambridge countryside. We'd drive and walk and stay at some small pub. It was because we got to know each other like that, that we wanted to be married. Sheila wanted children, so did I. She used to say that the most important thing any human being could do in life was to bring up a happy child. I had a wonderfully happy home. I agreed with her. We spent hours planning what we'd do with our family—we even chose names for our children— Sorry. I can't go on like this."

He put his head in his hands and began to sob. Pusey got up and put his hand on his shoulder. "Don't be ashamed of crying," he said. "It is honourable to feel grief." Then he said, "I'm a rotten host. When you came I offered you a drink, and we haven't had it yet. Major Blair, the decanter's on that table by the window. Could you pour out three stiff drinks?"

I was glad enough of mine, and the whisky certainly seemed to help Kirby. "It's just like a nightmare," he said. "I keep on wanting to wake up." He took another mouthful of whisky. "But I know it isn't a bad dream," he went on. "And I'm not really as soppy as I must have seemed a few minutes ago. I'm inclined to believe you when you say that Sheila was Edna Brown. But I *know* the whole of that letter is a damned lie. Sheila could never have written it. She wanted life for her baby—our baby—not death. I don't know why she didn't tell me about it, but she didn't. If only she had...." He was silent again for a long minute. "But she didn't. Why, I don't know. I *do* know that she wouldn't have been unhappy when she found that she was pregnant— she would have been delighted. We were going to be married in January, anyway. We could have got married any time she liked. Ours wasn't just an affair—we both knew it was for keeps. And I could no more have said what was in that letter than she could have hurt her baby's life. There's something desperately wrong."

"I think you should try to get some sleep," Pusey said. "I'll telephone for a cab.

"No, please don't," said Kirby. "I know the way to Victoria from here, and I'd rather walk. I've got a lot of thinking to do." He got up to go.

"May I come to see you in Cambridge—say tomorrow afternoon?" I said.

"Sure, any time," he answered. "I'm in Second Court at St James's. I could explain how to find my staircase, but it's a bit complicated. It will be easier for you to ask the porter at the gate, and he'll show you."

"I think that is a good idea," said Pusey. "Major Blair is a very discreet person, Mr Kirby, and it may be good for you to talk over things. May I ask you not to say anything about this for the present to anyone except Major Blair? Or, of course, me. I'll give you a number where you can get me."

He showed Kirby out, and came back to me. "I think we'll have another drink, Peter," he said. "Lord, I've got to Christian names already. Do you mind? I'm commonly called Ted. What do you make of it all?"

"I notice you said nothing about Gwen Rosing," I said. "How many other names did the girl have?"

"Goodness knows. I think we'll keep Gwen Rosing to ourselves, for a bit. I like that young man, Peter. He's going through hell, but he'll come out refined, not warped. And he could be very helpful. I'm not going to dictate what you say to him, but since you seem to have joined the Department remember the first law of the Department—never show your whole hand."

"I'll remember," I said.

"How did you get on with Miss Wilberforce?"

There hadn't been a chance to say much about her, and there didn't seem much to say. I gave him a report of our dinner party. When I mentioned that Miss Wilberforce said that she thought she had seen Mr Potterton somewhere before he broke in suddenly. "I'm not sure that that's not the most interesting thing yet."

"What on earth . . ."

"Brown and Cantilade, Peter, Brown and Cantilade, the owners of that famous typing pool. Before the scandal, when Rupert Hare was still a name to conjure with in the City, Brown and Cantilade were his solicitors."

5

Cambridge

I TELEPHONED CAMBRIDGE from my hotel, and booked a room for the night at the University Inn. I rang Pusey to let him know where I would be staying, but a woman told me that he was at a meeting. She seemed to know all about me, however, took my message, and told me not to forget to telephone again from Cambridge before I left.

There was a train that would get me to Cambridge just after four o'clock, and I felt that would be about right for clocking-in at the hotel and finding my way to Kirby at St James's College. Having nothing else to do that morning I went to the Westminster Public Library to see if Pusey was in *Who's Who*. He was,

Pusey, Edmund St. Clair, C.M.G.

He was five years older than me, and had gone straight from school into the Army, ending up as a Captain, with an M.C. He'd gone to Oxford on coming out of the Army, read philosophy and achieved a major university prize. Then he'd joined the Foreign Office, and served in various posts abroad before being transferred to the Home Office some four years ago. His foreign service no doubt explained the C.M.G. A transfer from the Foreign Office to the Home Civil Service is unusual, but Edmund Pusey was an unusual man. I was immensely impressed by him, particularly by his instant grasp of detail—the L.C. on the locket, the possible significance of Miss Wilberforce's Brown and Cantilade. I was also impressed, and not a little surprised, by his attitude to me. He seemed to regard me as at least an honorary member of his team. He had taken a quick decision to be frank—or fairly frank—with Kirby, and he'd taken an equally quick decision to trust me. It was his capacity for decision, perhaps, that had put him where he was. I could see, though, what George meant when he described his set-up as informal. It would be all right as long as the decisions were good ones. If he had a run of bad luck ... Well, that wasn't my business.

St James's is one of the older Cambridge colleges, approached through a splendid Tudor gateway, where there is a porter's lodge. I inquired for Mr Simon Kirby, and the porter came out to give me directions. To get to Second Court you walked quite logically through First Court, but after that the way became eccentric. The next block you came to was called Cleves Court—commemorating, apparently, a benefaction from Anne of Cleves—and then you had to negotiate Pillar Row. The porter, however, was experienced in explaining these intricacies, and I duly came to a staircase with a board indicating that Simon Kirby lived on the first floor. I went up and knocked.

The door opened so quickly that he might have been standing behind it to await me, as, perhaps, he was. He looked tired and strained, but he was clearly pleased that I had come. Would I like tea, or sherry—he was afraid he didn't have any whisky. It was just after five-thirty. A bit early for sherry, perhaps? I settled for tea, and he went into a small kitchen adjoining his sitting room to make it.

His quarters seemed palatial—sitting room, kitchen, and through another open door I could see a bedroom. All the walls were panelled in dark oak. "What marvellous rooms!" I said.

"Yes, the older part of the College gives you plenty of space," he replied. "But you have to walk something like a hundred and forty yards to get to a lavatory. And the central heating is more interesting as a piece of English social history than as a source of warmth. I have a post-graduate scholarship, which gives me a certain choice. I could live here, or have a smaller room with all mod. con. in one of the new buildings. For all the disadvantages, I'd rather be here."

"So would I," I said.

He brought the tea, and we sat down on a big leather couch.

"You don't look as if you've had much sleep," I said.

"I haven't had any. I still don't know what to believe. What *is* that house at Earl's Court?"

"It's let off in flats, or rather, rooms for typists and other girl office workers," I explained. "Four or five of them club together to rent a flat which none of them could possibly afford by herself. Edna Brown had a room there in a group organised by Miss Wilberforce, whom you met."

"Did she know her well?"

"Scarcely at all, I think. When one girl leaves the vacancy is advertised and another girl comes. It's a very casual arrangement. Miss Wilberforce knew Edna Brown as a girl who'd answered an advertisement and come to live there, and from whom she'd collected the rent. And she knew her to exchange a few words when they met in the hall, or in a communal sitting room that the girls have, but which doesn't seem to be used much. She knew nothing at all about her private life."

"Do *you* think that Edna Brown was Sheila?"

I didn't answer at once. Then I said, "My views aren't worth very much. I have never seen your Sheila, and I only saw Edna Brown after she was dead. And I was more concerned then with getting her body out of the sea and going for help than studying what she looked like. But—yes, I think they must have been the same. They lived at the same address. No one else has disappeared, there's no one else unaccounted for. And Miss Wilberforce, who knew Edna Brown well enough by sight, recognised her from your photograph. There's one other thing which might clinch matters. Did your Sheila ever wear a locket?"

"Yes, she did. She almost always wore it, a rather beautiful old Victorian locket of quite heavy gold. I used to tease her about it sometimes, but she never let me open it."

"Then I'm afraid there isn't any doubt at all. Just such a locket was found with Edna Brown."

He got up and walked over to the window, where he stood looking down into the nearly-dark courtyard, peaceful and secure, centuries removed from sudden death. Then he gave a sort of shudder, drew the window curtains and switched on the light.

"I've tried to think it isn't true," he said, "but it's no good. What do I do now? I can't even go to her funeral."

"You can help to secure justice."

He looked at me sharply. "What do you mean? And just how do you come to be mixed up in all this? I mean—you found her body, yes. But people who just find bodies don't normally go around with the police, or whoever they are, as you seem to be doing."

"Mr Kirby," I said, "there's a lot that you will have to take on trust. Can *you* be trusted?"

"I don't know what you want to trust me with. I can't say until I know. I'm beginning to wonder if *I* ought to go to the police."

I took a leaf out of Pusey's book and came to a decision. "I don't blame you," I said. "Would you like to ring up Metropolitan Police Headquarters—I won't give you the number, you'll find it in the London telephone book so there can't be any tricks—and ask to be put in touch with Commander Seddon of the CID?"

He shrugged. "No," he said. "If I have to believe the rest is true, I'll have to believe you. It's only that I don't *want* to believe any of it. I'm sorry. I'm not being very polite. You have taken a lot of trouble to come down here. I ought to be grateful."

"You'd do better to feel hatred," I said, "but not for me. If you'll listen to me for a little longer I think you'll understand." I gave him a slightly edited account of my bomb, and of the police suspicions that Edna Brown had been killed because of something she knew, perhaps relating to the drug traffic. "So you see," I concluded, "I have a very personal interest in getting to the bottom of it all."

"Thank you, Major Blair," he said rather formally. "Now I see what you mean by asking if I could be trusted. Yes, you *can* trust me." He held out his hand, and we solemnly shook hands.

He had not shown the surprise I had expected when I hinted at drugs.

"How did you come to meet Miss Mortimer?" I asked.

"At a party," he said. "But it wasn't quite an ordinary party. It was commercial, really. It was held in a room at the Golden Stars hotel to promote the direct sale of books to students. There was a notice on the College notice board, and I went along. The idea is that instead of going to a bookshop you order whatever you want from Knowledge Exchange—that's the name of the concern. They'll try to get you copies secondhand, which is much cheaper than buying new, and they undertake to buy them back from you at half the price you paid. If they have to send you a new book, you pay the ordinary price, but again there's the guarantee that they'll buy it back. They pay all the postage, whether they send books to you, or you're sending back to them. With text books as expensive as they are, it's a good scheme, and several of us have used it. Sheila was the demonstrator or saleswoman at that introductory party. I thought she was stunning, and when the thing was over I asked if I could take her out to dinner. I didn't think I had a hope, but she said Yes. I've got a car, and we went to a place at Grantchester. I was bowled over. She said she'd be coming back to Cambridge every other week or so for a bit, to collect orders, and see how the scheme was going. I asked if I could meet her next time she came, and again she said Yes. Then we got into the habit of seeing each other, and she started coming down at weekends. But she never actually came to Cambridge at weekends—she said that would be like work. She had her own Mini, and I'd meet her at Newmarket, or Saffron Walden, or somewhere. She'd leave her car there, and we'd go off together in mine."

"Do you know anybody who takes drugs?" I asked.

"Major Blair," he said, "I'm a geologist, but I'm a scholar of this college, and I'm not altogether a fool. I can see the implications of all that you have been saying only too well. There *was* a certain amount of mystery about Sheila, and if she went by another name in London, there's more mystery still. I loved Sheila as much as you can love anyone, and if she's alive I still love her. If she turned up tonight I'd marry her tomorrow, and we'd clear up the mystery afterwards. But I can't pretend that there weren't things that sometimes worried me. I didn't like not being allowed to go to her house, for instance.

"To answer your question. No, I don't actually know anyone who's on drugs. I know that drug-taking exists in Cambridge, as I suppose it does in a lot of other places. But you get a wrong impression from newspapers. Most undergraduates certainly *don't* take drugs. They come up to work. These are the men I know. I'm what some people would call a 'square'. I play squash, I row for the College, and I work damned hard. Of course other things go on here, but they're not my business. I can say with absolute certainty that Sheila herself didn't take any sort of drug. If she was mixed up in anything she was pushed into it. And if I can kill the people who pushed her, I will."

He spoke with a subdued intensity that I found deeply moving. I hoped I was right about him.

I realised that if I had guessed wrongly, the consequences for me were likely to be serious. If this intelligent young man was on the other side, they now knew, what so far they had only feared, that the locket had been found. They also knew that the police linked the dead girl, by whatever name she went under, with a ring of drug-pushers; that however smoothly, from their point of view, the inquest had appeared to go, the police file was by no means closed. But I had taken a calculated risk, as Pusey had, when he had told Kirby that he himself was not satisfied with the apparent findings of the inquest. God knows, one can make mistakes about people. But I had seen Kirby when Miss Wilberforce let him in, and I was convinced that he really was a puzzled young man, genuinely looking for his girl friend. His reaction to our conversation in his rooms had been natural, and more or less what one would expect, with the exception that he had shown neither anger, nor particular surprise, when I had mentioned drugs. But that, too, could be taken as a point in his favour. If he were a rogue, associated with his girl-friend in drug pushing, he would, I thought, have run for cover, expressing horror and indignation at the very idea that his girl could have been mixed up in anything so repulsive. He had obviously felt that there were aspects of her life that she wanted to hide, and he was too honest to pretend, to himself or to me, that they might not have been criminal. Anyway, I had recruited him as Pusey had apparently recruited me. This was a war which could not be fought without allies.

He asked again what he could do, and I said that hard as it was to have to live with one's thoughts, the best thing he could do for the present was to carry on as if nothing had happened. I asked him how many people knew of his relationship with Sheila. There would be very few, he thought. She had never been to the College, and from their first meeting they had never been together anywhere in Cambridge. He had taken her to visit his parents at Canterbury, and they would know that he felt seriously about her, but she had asked him not to tell them yet of their intention to get married, and he had not done so. That was one of the things that bothered him. He had wanted to announce their engagement, but she had begged him not to, and asked him not to give her a ring. She had used a curious phrase, not once, but on two or three occasions when they had been discussing their future. "I don't want anything to hurt our happiness," she had said. For a time he feared that she might be already married, and he had asked her point-blank about this. She had laughed, and said, "Lord, no."

As far as Kirby could see, her disappearance would not prompt any of his friends to ask questions—they had not done so yet, and he saw no reason why they should.

I asked him for all the details he could give me about Knowledge Exchange. He had first sent for some books, he said, because he thought it would help Sheila, but she had always seemed very detached about her job, and had never wanted to talk about it. He had gone on buying through Knowledge Exchange because they seemed efficient, and he reckoned to save money by using them. "Two books came at the end of last week," he said. "I've got them here, and the envelope they came in. You keep the envelopes and use them for sending back books that you want to sell." The books were two works on the geology of the oil industry, and the envelopes, of which he had several, were the big, padded sort that are made specially for sending books by post. With them was his latest invoice—a printed form headed Knowledge Exchange Limited, and giving an address in Gray's Inn Road. I asked if I could take the invoice and a couple of the envelopes. "Yes, certainly," he said. "I don't want the invoice. They send me a statement once a month, and you pay on that. If you've sent back any books during the month, they are credited to you. As I said, they seem a pretty efficient firm."

He asked if I'd like to stay for dinner in Hall, but I felt that it might be wiser for us not to be seen together. I did not tell him this, but said that I'd got some friends in Cambridge and had promised to look them up. "May I be an old soldier for a moment?" I said as we parted. "When you've got an objective, you must just carry on until you get there."

He said quietly, "I think I've got an objective now, Major Blair."

I telephoned Pusey at his flat at breakfast time and told him that I planned to take a train which would get me to Liverpool Street at 1103. He asked me to come straight to the Home Office, and I said I would.

He had Commander Seddon with him when I was shown into his room. "Charrington's looking after the President of Tintoroland," he said. "It's an awkward assignment. Having just expelled all Europeans from his country and expropriated their businesses, His Excellency is not all that popular here. The Foreign Office tactfully suggested that he might find the English climate more to his liking in the spring, but he took it as an insult to imply that an African ruler didn't have warm clothes, and said that he expected his visit to take place as arranged. It's a difficult world...

"Well, let's get down to our own business, Peter. How did you get on?"

I recounted my conversation with Simon Kirby, and gave him the Knowledge Exchange invoice and the book envelopes. He looked at them, and handed them to the CID man. "Your job, I think, Commander," he said. "There may be nothing in it, but there are some interesting possibilities. Regular postings, all open and above board, but the envelopes sent to some people contain more than books. If so, I wonder how they select them? The scheme would only work as long as most of the business was genuine.

"But it would explain La Rosing's somewhat excessive endowment of names. Edna Brown, P.R. girl for the advertising agency, often away, but established with a flat in London, insurance cards, and all the rest. Sheila Mortimer helping to run this rather ingenious scheme for selling books. If anybody ever thought of looking for Sheila Mortimer it would be pretty hard to find her. You'd hear of her in Cambridge and no doubt other university towns, but once she gets into her car and drives off, Sheila Mortimer doesn't exist. I wonder, I wonder.... We must certainly keep an eye on Knowledge Exchange."

The telephone rang, and Pusey answered it. "It's George," he said to me. "He wants to know if you are all right, and when you are coming back."

"Can I have a word with him?"

"Surely."

Pusey spoke into the telephone. "Hang on a moment, George," he said, "I've got Peter here."

I was considerably touched by George's solicitude. "Can I come back this evening?" I asked. "I haven't looked up trains yet, but I ought to be able to get one during the afternoon."

"There's a good train at three-fifteen from Paddington," George said. "It gets in around six. If you can get that, I'll meet you."

I thanked him, said I'd give him my news when we met, and rang off.

"We've got some news for you, Peter," Pusey said. "First, the boy Kirby. As far as we can check, everything he told us is true. He is the son of Canon Kirby, of Canterbury, apparently much respected, and well liked. Simon's record is a blameless one of academic achievement and minor success at sport—cricket at school, squash and rowing at Cambridge.

There's one sister, older than he is. She's a nurse at Manchester Royal Infirmary."

"I see," I said. "I wonder what you found out about me."

He laughed. "Second Rule of the Department, Peter—Nobody sees his own file." He went on, "I thought we'd better have a look at the letters he said were waiting for Sheila Mortimer at the newsagent's accommodation address. Paul Seddon arranged that. There were four, all from him. I won't read them out—it seems a sort of sacrilege. Extraordinary how being in love turns middle-class young Englishmen into poets, sometimes quite good poets. Kirby's letters to the girl are all high-grade love letters, getting more and more worried about her as time goes on, but not complaining. He clearly worshipped her, but in a decent dignified way. Pity she never got the letters... I suppose one day I shall have to ask him whether he wants them back. Maybe we can forget them, though. If he ever has to find out about Gwen Rosing there'll be more agony for him...."

He broke off, then continued, "Seddon's got news for you, too. He's found four curious messages in the personal columns of *The Examiner* which might relate to your code."

"They might," Seddon said, "but there seem to be too many figures. Here they are, anyway."

He handed me a sheet of typing paper. There were four lines on it. They read

Darling 0107902899511945 For Ever
For Ever 18002501339301610 Darling
Darling 12031134382681530 For Ever
For Ever 1115997176641907 Darling

The first had appeared on June 23 last year, the next on October 11, the third on March 4 this year and the last on July 12.

"There were a lot of papers to go through," Seddon said, "but the populars don't do much of this sort of thing—the cost per line with a circulation running into millions is prohibitive. *The Examiner* and *The Sentinel* seemed the best bet, but we went through all this year's files of the others as well, just in case. There wasn't anything that we could spot, nor did *The Sentinel* seem to have anything. When we found those two curious entries in *The Examiner* for July and March this year we went through last year's files as well, and came across the other two.

"Your code—if it is a code, or the key to a code—varies between eight and nine digits to a line. These vary between sixteen and seventeen. One would like to think that it was a simple numeral-letter code, with the figures in the messages standing for letters derived from the figures in the key. But there's no obvious relationship—in fact the differences in the number of digits rather seem to argue against any relationship. If you take the locket figures either by lines—eight or nine digits—or in total—fifty-nine digits—there is nothing to suggest any alphabetical relationship.

"There's another thing that argues against a numeral-letter code. If you look at the fourth message you'll see it begins 1-1-1. Now there's no word in English, or any other normal language, with the same letter occurring consecutively three times. You can get it spread over two words, like '*The eel*' or '... *Until Lloyds Bank* ...' but the combination is uncommon, and unlikely in a short message.

"Of course, digits may be paired, or read in other groups, to refer to words or phrases in a code-book. That seems slightly more likely here, but short of having a great deal more material, or some indication of the code-book, it's hard to see how one can get much farther.

"And, again, there's not the slightest evidence to indicate that the figures in the locket and the figures in these *Examiner* advertisements are connected in any way at all. But to say that there isn't any evidence to connect them may mean merely that we haven't found any evidence. We have found a piece of paper with rows of figures on it, which we believe to be connected in some way with criminal activities that would seem to require communications. We have now also found another series of so far inexplicable figures, which would, at least, fit in with what we might call '*the need to communicate*'. Whether they do or not, God knows, but obviously we can't dismiss them yet.

"The intervals between *The Examiner* advertisements—June, October, March, July—are not constant, but they suggest a rough periodicity within the range of four to five months. That, again, would fit in with the sort of traffic we are envisaging, with consignments of heroin being available for collection three times a year, or so. They wouldn't want to send consignments too often, but they would need them with some degree of regularity."

"What about the words in the advertisements?" I asked. "There are the 'Darlings' and 'For Evers' as well as the figures."

"Your guess is as good as anyone's," he said. "They are reversed in alternate messages, which suggests that one advertiser is replying to another, but there seems rather too long an interval between them for any sort of regular correspondence. They could be just indicators, to say that a message is meant for A rather than B. I can't offer anything better at present. But to get on with my story:

"I've been to see the advertisement director of *The Examiner*, and he called in the editor. Of course, I didn't say anything about drugs, or about Gwen Rosing, but I explained that we had some reason for thinking that those advertisements in their personal column might be associated with crime. I didn't actually say anything about spying, but one of them jumped to the idea of spying, and I didn't say it wasn't. Anyway, they both understood that the whole business came under the 'Most Secret' classification, and they were sufficiently excited to go to a lot of trouble for me.

"What they found was curious—all four advertisements came from their Paris office, and were paid for in cash. They were Telexed to London in the ordinary way, and nobody might have remembered much about them if one of the operators in the paper's London wire-room hadn't recalled asking for a repeat of the figures on the last message. That put them on to Paris, and the office then managed to trace the others through the cash-book. It is much more difficult to trace the sender. When you call at a branch office to put in one of these small advertisements you are given a form ruled off in squares for each word, and you put your name and address on a numbered counterfoil attached to the form. The message part of the form is torn off and goes to the Telex operator, and the counterfoil is supposed to provide a check if any query should arise. The trouble is that the copy for the messages is only kept for three months. That's considered long enough for all ordinary purposes, and I've no doubt it is, but it's awkward for us. In this case we had a bit of luck because of that repeated Telex. The operators log repeats, and the number of the Paris message was entered in the log-book. That enabled the Paris office to track down the counterfoil. I got the name and address from it last night, and I sent them off at once to the French police, asking them to find out what they could about the chap. I heard from them this morning—the address doesn't exist.

"I won't say that gets us no forrader, because it does bear out that the advertisements are mixed up with funny business of some sort. But it may be no more than a little light adultery."

"You've managed to find out a hell of a lot in very little time," I said. "I can't judge by CID standards because I don't know them, but it seems to me that you've done marvellously."

Seddon laughed. "I had two bits of luck," he said. "The advertisement director and the editor were both exceptionally intelligent men, and the repeated Telex was a godsend."

"What do we do now?" I asked.

"Carry on with the patient routine that in the end brings most results in life," Pusey said. "You've opened an interesting new line of inquiry at Cambridge."

"And the code?"

"All the cipher experts say that code with so little material is all but uncrackable," Seddon put in. "That doesn't mean we give up. I'm afraid it does mean that I don't at present feel very hopeful."

"What about the periodicity of *The Examiner* advertisements? Unless they belong to some affair that is now over and done with, one might expect another one fairly soon."

"We've thought of that," said Pusey. "Seddon has arranged with *The Examiner* people that if another one crops up, they'll let him know at once. Then we'll have to decide whether to ask them not to publish it—all newspapers have paragraphs in small print saying that the editor reserves the right not to publish advertisements without giving a reason, but it's not always easy to act on. In this case I think *The Examiner* would withhold the ad if we asked them to, but it might not be wise. If it just didn't appear, it would be a red light to all concerned. It might be better just to let it go ahead. I don't know yet. It's a hypothetical problem at the moment because there hasn't been another advertisement. We'll have to wait and see."

It was time for lunch, and I had to get to Paddington for my train. Pusey had a luncheon date somewhere and Seddon asked if I'd join him in a quick meal in the staff dining room on the premises. Before he went off, Pusey asked what I proposed to do. "Go back to Exeter and think about my troubles, I suppose," I said. "I don't know how long George can put up with me, and I really want to go home."

"I'll be in touch with you through George," he said, "but

ring me direct at any time you want to. Don't forget that there are some very nasty people around, and that you're not out of the wood yet."

I asked Seddon if I could have a copy of *The Examiner* advertisements. "Sure," he said, "have this." He gave me the sheet of paper, adding, "It's only a carbon copy, and I've two or three more in the file."

I put the paper in my wallet, and we went to lunch.

6

The Code

WHEN SYBIL WANTED to annoy me, she used to say that I had a crossword mind. By this she didn't mean that I wanted to sit at home and do crosswords when she wanted to go out—I hardly ever did them at home when I was living with her—but that I tend to complicate questions (such as the need for a fourth new dress in one week) that to her were transparently simple. Looking back, I'm inclined to admit that there was some truth in her charge. I *have* always enjoyed crossword puzzles, and I think that I do tend sometimes to look at things obliquely when it would be easier to be direct. But an oblique approach is not always a handicap.

I was fascinated by those four rows of figures. I bought a couple of magazines to read in the train, but I scarcely looked at them. Soon after we started a man came round announcing tea, and I went to the restaurant car. Breakfast and tea are, to my mind, the only meals worth having on an English train. Lunch and dinner may be necessary on some journeys, but one eats them merely to assuage hunger. Breakfast and tea—particularly on the Western Region of British Rail, which has inherited some of the noble tradition of the old Great Western Railway—are sheer delight. Where else in modern English life are you ever offered toasted teacakes and thin bread and butter at four o'clock? The train was half empty, and I had a table to myself. The early-winter day was darkening, and we ran through a landscape of gathering dusk. The lighted tea-table was intimate to me, and detached from the rest of the world. I enjoyed my tea-cake and pored over the figures.

Eight ... nine ... sixteen ... seventeen. Seddon was right, it was hard to see any sort of relationship between the locket figures and the figures in the advertisements. Sixteen was a multiple of eight. So what? And where did fifty-nine come into it? Mentally, I said the figures to myself in groups, like telephone numbers. 0107 ... 9028 ... 9951 ... 1945 ... I'd checked my train on the time-table displayed at Paddington, and been slightly annoyed with myself for having to convert the railways' twenty-four-hour notation into the familiar a.m. and p.m. 1945 might be a time ... I looked at the first and last groups of all four lines, 0107 ... 1945, 1800 ... 1610, 1203 ... 1530, 1115 ... 1907. I felt a sudden excitement. Yes, they could all be times. Suppose the figures weren't in code at all? Here we were, looking for a complicated code to crack, and perhaps the meaning was staring us in the face!

My elation died. The other groups wouldn't do. 9028, 9951, 2501.... These couldn't be times. And the seventeen-figure lines had too many figures; they wouldn't divide into groups of four.

But I couldn't get the thought out of my head. I abandoned the awkward middle figures and concentrated on what I was now calling to myself the "time-groups". Why would anyone want two times in one message? Was something supposed to happen between two times? If so, what sort of an interval was there?

The first message gave the best part of a whole day, from a few minutes after one o'clock in the morning to a quarter to eight in the evening. The second was tiresome; it almost seemed to go backwards, from six o'clock in the evening to ten minutes past four—of course, it could be from one evening to the afternoon next day, but I didn't like it. The remaining two were all right, from midday to half-past three in the afternoon, and from 11.15 in the morning to just after seven o'clock at night.

They were wildly different intervals. What on earth could be expected to happen over such eccentric periods? Arrivals and departures? Yes, that was possible. But the times were extraordinarily precise. 01.07 in one message, 12.03 in another, 19.07 in a third. I didn't like it.

Then another thought struck me: what about a date? 1945 was a possible year, but an impossible way of writing a day of the month. So were 1530, 1115 and 1800. The others would do—0107 = 1/7 = July 1, 1203 = 12/3 = March 12. Looking at the messages line by line, I saw that each message contained one possible date.

How did they fit with the dates of publication of the advertisements? The first appeared on June 23 last year, but the date in the message, 0107 = July 1, seemed to be the wrong month. What about the others—October 11, March 4 and July 12. And the dates in the messages, if they were dates, gave 1610 = October 16, 1203 = March 12, 1907 = July 19. The months were all right, with the dates in the messages a week or eight days ahead of the dates on which the messages had appeared. Damn that first date! I looked at it again. Yes, the thing had appeared on June 23, but the message date 0107 couldn't be a date in June, it must be July 1. A week ahead! Heavens, I'd got it! If the date were July 1, and it followed the pattern of the others, the message had to appear on or about June 23.

I felt a tremendous sense of triumph, intensified a moment later when I spotted something else—the reversals of "Darling" and "For Ever". When the message began "Darling" the date-group was at the beginning: when it began "For Ever" the date-group was at the end! So it worked—a date and a time in each message, and an indicator to tell you which was which in case of any confusion (as there could be with 0107, for instance).

The triumph didn't last. It was all very well to have dug dates and times out of these sets of figures, but I was no nearer knowing what was supposed to happen on those dates and times. And it was all guess work, anyway. My dates and times might be no more than arithmetical coincidence. I was beginning to feel thoroughly miserable, when to my astonishment the train drew into Exeter. At least my playing about with figures had made the journey pass quickly.

George was waiting at the barrier, and we got into his car. "You seem to have had a profitable time," he said as we drove off. "Pusey didn't tell me much, but he seems very pleased with you. He says you're to be regarded as a member of the Department."

"Acting, unpaid.... It's like the Army all over again!" I laughed. "But he was jolly nice to me, George. Mainly because of you, I think."

"Come off it! Anyway, I'm glad it turned out all right. I was a bit bothered about putting up a black by taking you along. These high-ups are nice and polite, and they tell you to be informal, but they don't always welcome too much informality."

On the way to Topsham I told George about Miss Wilberforce and Simon Kirby, but I couldn't show him the messages in the car, and we were still discussing Simon Kirby when we got to George's house. Mary was as welcoming as ever, but there had to be an interval for drinks and a meal before I could get on with my story. After supper George took me into his study, and we were able to get down to things. I told George Commander Seddon's story of the advertisements, and I gave him Seddon's paper, making a copy of the messages for myself. I didn't tell him of my thoughts on dates and times.

"It boils down to this," George said. "With some luck—and some wonderful initiative by you, Peter—we've established that there really was a girl organising a sort of mail-order service at Cambridge that may or may not have been used for distributing heroin. Paul Seddon has no doubt got a team of people going into all this now. They'll find out everything they can about Knowledge Exchange, discover if, and how, it operates in other universities, and keep an eye on its parcels. That's the sort of plodding work that gets results, but it takes time. I'll have a go at Exeter tomorrow—see if the Knowledge Exchange service has got here.

"On the face of things, it seems a highly dubious business. If it's above board, why should the girl call herself Sheila Mortimer when she was supposed to be working for an advertising agency as Edna Brown? Of course, it may have been some quite ordinary little swindle on her part—fiddling two lots of expenses, or something. We don't know yet, but it looks suspicious. It also explains why we were never able to pin down any of the rather vague rumours that reached us that Gwen Rosing was mixed up in the thing. The Sheila Mortimer existence—or non-existence—was a good trick.

"As for the figures in the locket and the messages in *The Examiner*—again we don't know. The chances are that they've nothing to do with one another. We may never find out. Pusey can get hold of the best cryptographers in Britain, but they've precious little to work on. All we can do here is to wait and see."

"If you are right about dinghy-smuggling," I said, "and the more I think of it the more I reckon that there is—or could be—something in it, then they'd need a code of some sort."

"Why? Why couldn't the smuggler make arrangements in the East, fly back in advance of the ship and pick her up in the Channel?"

"There would be practical difficulties," I answered, "Particularly if the operation had to be repeated two or three times a year. And the last thing they'd want would be any traceable connection with the ship, or the shipping line, or the agents, or whatever. As I see it, there'd be no need for the smuggler ever to go on board the ship. It wouldn't stop in the Channel —stopped ships get seen, and other seamen wonder what is happening. No, they'd try to make the fact that there are plenty of ships and small boats about in the Channel into a safeguard. The ship would have to be sure that the right dinghy was around, but it wouldn't have to come all that close—it could be identified through glasses. Then they'd throw a buoyed package overboard—the chap in the dinghy could also be observing through glasses. In fog or heavy weather they could call off the whole operation. But to arrange a drop successfully they'd need communications. There'd have to be advance notice that the ship would be in a given position at a given date and time. I like the idea of using *The Examiner*'s personal column for this. As Seddon found, it's easy enough to hide the identity of whoever puts in such an advertisement. And since it can be read by anyone, there's no direct link of any sort with the person it's intended for."

George considered this. "You may be right," he said, "but it will be a hell of a job to prove it."

I changed the subject a bit. "What do you suppose Pusey meant," I asked, "by saying that Miss Wilberforce's feeling that she'd seen the advertising man—Potterton—somewhere or other might be important?"

"I don't know, Peter," George said. "Pusey has got a remarkable mind, a sort of living combination of a computer and a card-index. Remember how he trotted out the name of Gwen Rosing's great-grandmother? The Rosing girl keeps cropping up in all this business, but we haven't any clear idea of just how she fits in. She was attractive, and apparently very clever, but somehow I don't see her master-minding an international drug-ring. Her old boy-friend, or protector, Rupert Hare is very different. But he hopped out of the way quickly when the Whitehall scandal broke, and as far as we know he's still somewhere in South America, and likely to stay there. The firm of solicitors Miss Wilberforce works for may well have acted for him at some time—that's just the sort of knowledge Pusey would have at his finger-tips. He may have meant no more than that any link with the Rosing girl and Hare, however remote and tenuous now, is interesting."

"I see," I said.

George's house has good central heating, and my bedroom was warm enough to sit in in pyjamas. I couldn't sleep, so I sat at the dressing-table and had another look at the messages. Random sets of four figures may produce possible dates and times, but if you are looking for messages conveying dates and times, and you find figures in a message that can be read as dates and times, you can't easily dismiss them as coincidence. I'd been through triumph and despair over these figures, and was now back to eagerness. I didn't rate myself a cryptographer in the sense of the experts on whom Pusey could call. Seddon obviously had a considerable knowledge of cryptography, but this meant that he approached a code in the expert way of looking for repeated figures or groups of figures that might suggest the most frequently used letters, words, or phrases. The experts were quite right in saying that without having a lot of messages to compare with one another, any code can be more or less uncrackable. But they think in terms of proper codes with elaborate code books, used for sending long messages between ambassadors and such-like.

I didn't think the locket-code was like that at all. And the short *Examiner* messages didn't look like an elaborate code, either. I'd worked out in my own mind just what sort of information a heroin agent would have to send to a dinghy smuggler, and it didn't amount to more than three things—

date, time, and position. If my date and time-groups were right, they could be sent in clear. If the position-figures were jumbled, and the date and time figures tacked on to them, you'd get a line of incomprehensible figures—precisely what we had.

Knocking off the date and time groups from the first message left

90289951

Eight figures—that would fit with latitude and longitude in degrees and minutes. I had no atlas in the bedroom, but my diary had a set of maps of the world. The scale was tiny, and, of course, hopeless for plotting an actual position, but the maps did show me roughly the part of the world positions would be in. 90.28 was an impossible latitude, since 90.00 would be the North Pole (or possibly the South Pole). I tried reading the figures backwards

15.99 N (or S) 82.09 W (or E)

That put us roughly in Central America, or India, or Peru or in the middle of the Indian Ocean, depending on whether I made the figures read North or South—East or West. None seemed to make any sense.

If they were position-figures, I concluded they must be coded ones. Could I use the locket-figures as a key? Well, I could try, anyway. I could divide or multiply, add or subtract. Division and multiplication offered no hope of sensible figures so I didn't bother with them. I took the first line of the locket-figures, 50167309, and added it to the first of the message-figures (excluding the date and time groups). That produced 140457260—nine figures, with an impossible latitude. I wondered if positions might be given, perhaps, in degrees, minutes and seconds. But that would need twelve figures, and I didn't see a dinghy navigating anywhere within seconds, so I ruled that out. Subtracting gave a reasonably possible position 40.12 26.42, but 40 deg N latitude would put us in the middle of the North Atlantic, S latitude in the middle of the South Atlantic, and since I was looking for somewhere within dinghy-reach of Devon or Cornwall, neither seemed any good.

There were seven rows of locket figures, and I decided to try them all. It meant a horrible lot of arithmetic, but I had all night ahead of me. Since adding seemed to produce impossible figures I concentrated on subtracting. When I worked out the sum for the fourth row of locket-figures my heart jumped a beat. The subtraction left

    50.10 03.40

Even from my tiny diary map I could see that 50.10 N 03.40 W put one nicely in the Channel, within comfortable sailing distance of Start Point.

But why the *fourth* line of the locket-figures? Were there three earlier messages that we'd missed, so that the first message in our collection was really the fourth in some sequence relating to the locket figures. If so, the second message should be the fifth. I tried subtracting the fifth line of the locket-figures from the second line of message-figures, again excluding what seemed to be the date and time groups. It didn't work—it gave a nine-figure answer. I wrote out all the locket-figures again, and pored over them:

5016	7309	(8 figures)
2000	13530	(9 ,,)
1827	10550	(9 ,,)
4018	9611	(8 ,,)
6332	7918	(8 ,,)
5123	0231	(8 ,,)
3219	10728	(9 ,,)

I needed a nine-figure line from the locket-table, so I tried the last line. That didn't work either—the locket-figure was bigger than the message figure, and I couldn't subtract it. I tried another nine-figure line—the second line of the locket-table. That came out splendidly again

    50.12 04.00

Assuming North latitude and West longitude as before, that gave another position in the Channel highly convenient to the Devon coast. I was sure I was on to it, but I hadn't mastered the code. How *did* the wretched thing work? How could the reader of a message tell which line of the locket-figures to use? It couldn't be the number of digits in a line because that sometimes gave impossible sums. Go on trying until you came to a line that did work? It seemed a tiresome way of decoding a message, and I didn't believe that the people who had shown such ingenuity in devising the code would have left such an untidy loose end.

I turned from the locket-figures to the messages. There *must* be some key in those. Could it be the positioning of "*Darling*" and "*For Ever*"? No, one message which began with "*Darling*" had eight figures between the date and time groups, the other nine. It must be something else. But how else did the messages differ? The dates and times were different. How about the date?

Suddenly it struck me that there were seven rows of figures in the locket-table—and seven days in a week. I looked in my diary—damn, this year's diary was no good. But there was a last year's calendar at the end. I looked up that, and found that July 1 was a Saturday. October 19, the date—or what I had elucidated as the date—in the second message was a Thursday. I wrote the days against the lines in the locket-table that had given me what I felt were good results

	5016 7309
Thursday	200013530
	182710550
Saturday	4018 9611
	6332 7918

5123 0231
321910728

And then I had it! Thursday and Saturday came in the right sequence! I wrote in the rest of the days,

Wednesday	50167309
Thursday	200013530
Friday	182710550
Saturday	40189611
Sunday	63327918
Monday	51230231
Tuesday	321910728

Then I tried the other messages, March 12 (a Sunday) and July 19 (a Wednesday) against what I reckoned to be the "Sunday" and "Wednesday" lines in the locket-figures, and both gave positions in the Channel nicely near the Devon coast. I wondered why it was necessary to complicate the code by having seven different cipher-lines, but I soon saw that there would be a considerable risk of figures repeating themselves if they didn't. Assuming that the dinghy worked out of the Salcombe estuary or somewhere nearabouts, it would have only a small area of Channel to work in. They might try to vary the minutes, but it was quite likely that at least the degrees of latitude and longitude would have to be the same for different drops, and in the small area involved even the minutes might not vary much. By varying the cipher-lines the possibility of 'repeats", which might give a clue to any undesirable person studying the messages, was greatly reduced.

I was so excited as soon as I was satisfied that I'd broken the code that I rushed straight to George's room. I flung open the door and turned on the light. George and Mary were sleeping peacefully. George sat up in bed with a shout of "What the hell...!"

"I've got it, I've got it," I said. "I can read the messages."
It was not quite 4 a.m.

George insisted on getting up and making coffee. I collected the scraps of paper covered with figures from my dressing table, and we went to his study. It took a little time to explain the workings. George listened in utter silence, and then worked out all four messages himself. He got an atlas, and confirmed that the positions were all in the right part of the Channel, precisely, in fact, where one would expect them to be if his theory of dinghy-smuggling had hit upon the truth. I thought that now there could be no doubt about this.

George was more cautious. "I grant that these coded messages make it seem much more likely," he said. "But we haven't any evidence that they relate to dinghy-smuggling. Or to heroin, for that matter."

"The code came from the locket," I reminded him, "and the locket from a girl you believe to have been mixed up with heroin."

"Oh yes. I'm only being a policeman." He laughed a little, but quickly became serious again. "There's a fearful lot still to be done," he went on. "If you've got those messages right, when was the last delivery?"

"July 12—this year," I said.

"Getting on for five months ago. Not much hope of tracing the stuff now, it will all have been distributed. At least we've a line on *how* it may have been distributed. Let me see—there's a train soon after six. I must go up to London straight away and tell Pusey about this. Will you come?"

I suddenly felt overwhelmingly sleepy. It was after five, and we'd have to get dressed and leave for Exeter almost straight away. "Do you mind if I don't?" I said. "You can say everything that I could. I'm feeling desperately tired, and if Mary doesn't mind I'd like to spend most of the morning in bed."

"You've certainly earned it," George replied.

Mary made me stay in bed until George came home. He caught the same train that I'd got yesterday, and was in soon after seven. I heard him come in, had a quick bath and went down. I felt much refreshed.

Back in the now familiar study after supper, George poured me what seemed an excessively large quota of whisky, and one of much the same size for himself. "You don't need me to tell you how pleased Pusey is," he said. "And Seddon is just as excited. He *could* have been a bit put out, you know. He's a professional, and you breeze in and solve the puzzle. But if he felt a trace of that, he didn't show it. He's one of the most genuinely dedicated men I've met in the police force. What was it we learnt at school? *Fiat justitia, ruat coelum.* Seddon's got no side. He's all for anything and anybody who helps to get justice done."

"Seddon's got nothing to reproach himself for," I said. "He was looking for a proper code, and given a high-grade cipher he'd be a hundred times more use than I am. I simply worked out what I'd need if I were dinghy-smuggling, and went backwards from that. The rest was luck."

"Well, luck or no, it was a most impressive job," George said.

"What is the plan of campaign now?" I asked.

"Seddon and Co. are burrowing away, and will go on burrowing," George replied. "The code, in a sense, has brought the other side of things rather to a standstill. I mean, we can read the messages we have, but they're all past messages. They tell us *how* things were done, but they don't tell us what is going to happen next. There may not be any more messages. They may feel that the Rosing girl's death has compromised things, and decide that they've got to change the system."

"We don't know why Gwen Rosing was killed," I said.

"No," said George, "but one can begin to make a fair guess. A lot still has to be assumption, but they're becoming reasonable assumptions. We can assume that she was mixed up in this heroin ring, deeply mixed up in it. We know now that in another context she was in love—apparently quite genuinely in love—with your pal Simon Kirby. We know that she was going to have a child, and—again apparently—that she wanted to have a child. She could have told her people that she wanted to get out, and they may have felt that she was too dangerous to let go. There is a hell of a lot we still don't know—we don't know why it was so important for them that she should be found and identified as Edna Brown."

"I'm with you so far," I said. "She had an appalling childhood, and she was still not much more than a kid. But kids grow up. I know heredity is unfashionable nowadays, but I keep thinking of a remark of Pusey's when he was telling us about her mother. She appears to have been a pretty promiscuous sort, but she hung on to her daughter, and seems to have done what she could for her. Maybe Gwen had the same kind of instincts, combining promiscuity with genuine maternal feeling. That may be commoner among women than we realise, only most of them are so shuttered-in by society that the less respectable instincts get suppressed. Gwen had an utterly uninhibited early life. She may have felt that she'd had enough, and—though she probably didn't reason it out—that she really wanted to mother somebody. Quite possibly she wanted to mother young Kirby as well as his child. You say that we don't know why whoever killed her was so anxious that she should die as Edna Brown and not as Gwen Rosing. I think we can make a fair guess at that, too."

"Why?" asked George.

"Publicity, first, perhaps," I went on. "You can imagine

the storm of newspaper and TV publicity that would have broken if the unknown and uninteresting Edna Brown had turned out to be the notorious and exceedingly interesting Gwen Rosing. Every newspaper in Britain would have had men out trying to discover where she'd been, what she'd been doing, why she called herself Edna Brown. In the course of all this someone might easily have stumbled on something relating her to the heroin-ring. That's the obvious explanation, and it's probably explanation enough. But there's still more to it. They didn't want the public to know that the dead girl was Gwen Rosing, but equally they didn't want the police to know. They may not have known that you had any idea that Gwen Rosing was mixed up with them."

"I don't see how they could have known," George put in. "I don't under-rate their intelligence, but it's most unlikely that suspicions within Pusey's set-up could have leaked."

"Yes, and I think the attacks on me bear that out," I said. "If you knew all about the Rosing girl already, why go to a lot of trouble to murder me?"

"Okay," George said. "But I don't know where that gets us."

I had a half-plan, which I now brought out.

"It seems to me," I said, "that your efforts to cloud the inquest on Edna Brown worked out badly in at least one direction. Sure, you didn't disclose your hand, and you kept the enemy guessing, but you didn't let the inquest do any real probing. Nobody asked Mr Potterton anything, except to identify the girl as Edna Brown who had worked for him. Who exactly is Mr Potterton? Why does he keep a yawl at Salcombe? Why, indeed, did Edna Brown choose Salcombe for her somewhat dramatic exit from the world? There are lots of places nearer London where she could have drowned herself. What's wrong with the Thames?"

"She was going for a walking tour on Dartmoor," said George. "That hung together."

"What did it hang with? The story that she was going to have a holiday and then drown herself! But we don't believe she did drown herself—if half the story is bogus, why not the other half?" I had been thinking a lot about all this. "Look, George," I went on, "you and Mary have been awfully good to me, but I want to get home. And I've thought of a way of combining this with establishing closer relations with Mr Potterton."

I explained my idea. Mr Potterton ran an advertising agency. I was developing a furniture making business. I could write to Mr Potterton saying that I had fairly ambitious plans for the future, and asking if his agency would be willing to look after my advertising. If everything about Mr Potterton were straightforward, nothing would be lost—I might even get a few customers. If things were not wholly what they seemed, I might manage to pick up some bits of useful information.

"Suppose he says that he is sorry, but you are too small—that he only handles accounts over so many thousands of pounds a year?" George observed.

"He won't," I said. "It's not so long since I was a marketing tycoon, and I know what to say to an advertising agency."

We turned to discussing my proposal to go home. George was not happy about this. "You're a free agent," he said, "and short of arresting you on suspicion—and I'm not sure that you haven't given us grounds for this—I can't stop you. But in all the excitement of the past few days you seem to have forgotten that you're a target as well as a detective. There's been one devilishly ingenious attempt on your life, and there's no saying when there won't be another. You're in just as much danger now as you were before the bomb went off—perhaps more, because having failed to get you once they may be more successful next time."

This was very much in my mind, and I can't pretend I

wasn't worried. But it seemed to me that time might be a little on my side. Murder is at best an inconvenient business, and however skilfully carried out entails at least some risk for the murderer. The attempt on my life could have been made only for some knowledge supposed to have been in my possession. Either it was not in my possession, in which case there was no point in continuing to go after me, or I might have been so thoroughly frightened that I'd keep my mouth shut. The fact that—from the murderer's point of view—nothing had happened since he'd sent his bomb might reasonably suggest that one or other of my arguments—again from his point of view—was valid. I put these points to George. He didn't think much of them, but he did think quite highly of my plan for getting in touch with Mr Potterton. "As a policeman," he said, "I've enjoyed reading about Sherlock Holmes, but outside books I've never come across a lay detective who was the slightest use for anything except collecting the more obvious sort of evidence in divorce cases. I'm not flattering you, Peter, but you're different—you're in the case anyway, and you've been able to do things, like taking Miss Wilberforce out to dinner, which it would be hard for a regular policeman to do, at any rate naturally. And your luck, or, to be more polite, your habit of thinking from one thing to another, is enough to make any policeman jealous. You can get Mr Potterton to talk to you in a way that he wouldn't talk to me, or to Seddon—if only because you can lie with a clear conscience in a way that we can't. But I don't like it. I'm paid to take a certain amount of risk; you're not."

"We've both been in the Army, George," I reminded him.

"Oh, to hell with it! We'll do what we can to keep an eye on you, but you can't have a bodyguard all the time, so it can only be a limited protection. I'll tell you one thing—you're not going back to that cottage of yours until you've had a telephone put in."

"But I don't want a telephone. One of the reasons I'm living in the cottage is to get away from telephones."

"Well, you can't have a convincing furniture business without a telephone."

That, I admitted, was a point. George said that he had official links with the Post Office by which he could get a telephone installed in half a day, and I agreed not to go back until the phone was in. "But we don't know if the place is fit to live in yet," he said. I said that my bedroom was more or less undamaged, and that I had some tables and chairs in my workshop. "If the police are all powerful with the Post Office," I added, "maybe Sergeant Manning could persuade a glazier to put some glass in the windows, if necessary."

That settled things. George said that he'd get in touch with the Post Office in the morning, and I began designing letter-heads for "Peter Blair, Cabinet Maker".

7

I Meet Mr Potterton

GEORGE HAD NOT exaggerated his pull with the Post Office, and by midday I'd not only been promised a phone within twenty-four hours but told what my number would be. I had mixed feelings about the phone itself, fearing that once the thing was installed I'd never get around to having it removed, but George was right about the need for a telephone number on my letter to Mr Potterton. I had an unexpected bonus from the CID here, too. George got one of his staff to telephone a local printer, who had my letterheads ready for me that same evening.

I wrote:

Dear Mr Potterton,

Please forgive my writing to you without an introduction, and on the very slightest of acquaintance—formed, moreover, in most distressing circumstances. You may recall that we both gave evidence at a recent inquest on a young woman whose body was washed ashore near Salcombe.

I noted then that you are a director of a London advertising agency, and being much in need of skilled advice on publicity I am emboldened to write this letter to you.

I have recently started a small business in the making and selling of high-grade cottage furniture. This has proved so successful that I am planning to extend it, but

I want, if possible, to continue to supply customers direct. I make high-grade, and, inevitably, rather expensive furniture, and it seems to me that I might wisely invest a considerable amount of my available capital in selective advertising. This is where I need advice. Would your agency be willing to handle such publicity for me, and both plan and place the advertising that I feel I need for the development of my business?

       Yours sincerely,
        Peter Blair.

George had a copy of the depositions at the inquest, and I got the agency's address from there. It was called Angus Potterton Associates, and the address in Half Moon Street, off Piccadilly, certainly sounded a posh one. I wasn't dissatisfied, though, with my own letterheading, which, with the printer's help, had come out in a way that I thought quite impressive. George's secretary typed my letter for me, and I posted it in Exeter the day before I went home.

Mrs Moss's daughter had turned up trumps. The builder she worked for had put new glass in all my broken windows, and re-plastered the sitting room walls and ceiling. The whole place still needed decorating, but that could wait. It was habitable again as it was.

George and Mary had been the most considerate of hosts, but I was thankful to be home: living in someone else's house, even with the best of friends, is always rather a strain. The telephone was in my sitting-room, with an extension in my bedroom, and beside both instruments was an inconspicuous button which rang an alarm in Kingsbridge police station without having to get through on the phone. I'd not been in the house many minutes when Sergeant Manning called to see me. He was less cheerful than usual. "It's good to see you back, Major Blair," he said, "but I can't help feeling that you're a fearful responsibility. You're a bit like a Royal Visit that goes on all the time."

I told him not to worry, though both of us knew that the words rang somewhat hollow. He asked me to let the police station know in advance of all my movements, and, whenever I went out, to give an estimated time when I expected to get home. He explained about the phone-button, and promised that if I ever needed to press it the nearest police car would come at once. I thanked him, and meant it.

When he'd gone I went over the whole cottage looking for booby-traps, but found nothing that seemed out of place. I can't say that I enjoyed my first night back, but I bolted everything and told myself that life was not going to be worth living if I was frightened all the time. My only weapon was the sword I'd had in the Army. Feeling slightly ridiculous, I drew it from its scabbard and put it by my bed. A man rushing down with a drawn sword should, I felt, at least be upsetting to an intruder. I didn't dwell on the relative efficiency as weapons of my sword and an automatic pistol.

The night, however, passed without incident, and in the morning I felt better, thoroughly enjoying the breakfast that I was able to cook for myself and eat without having to make polite conversation. I set to work on repainting my walls, and decided that I might as well do up the whole cottage while I was about it. That gave me something to do and kept my mind off things.

On my third day at home there was a letter in an envelope printed "Angus Potterton Associates". It was my first letter since my bomb, and I handled it gingerly. I held it up to the light, and there seemed to be nothing inside but a normally folded piece of paper. I decided to go outside to open it, so that if there was to be an explosion it would not be in a confined space. I had to grit my teeth to slit the envelope, and felt almost let down when nothing happened at all.

The letter was remarkably friendly.

> Dear Mr Blair (it said)
>
> I am most interested in your letter, and am very glad that you wrote. Our Agency rather specialises in what, I think, is very much your sort of business—selective selling in limited but high-grade markets. I have a number of suggestions which you might consider, and I shall be delighted to discuss them with you.
>
> I am a keen sailor myself and for some time I have kept a yawl in Salcombe harbour, so I am quite often in your part of the world (although, alas, not as often as I should like). I'm not sure that we haven't exchanged waves occasionally on the water.
>
> I am, in fact, coming down this weekend. Could you meet me for lunch at the Corinthian Yacht Club on Saturday? Don't bother to telephone here—if you ring the club and leave a message I shall get it when I come. I greatly hope that we can meet as I suggest.
>
> Yours sincerely,
> Angus Potterton

The Corinthian is one of the newer clubs which have grown up with the vast increase in dinghy sailing since the Second World War, and it caters primarily for dinghy sailors as distinct from the owners of cruising and ocean-racing yachts. It has enough members who sail all the year round to keep its bar and dining room open in winter. I was not myself a member of it—my father had belonged to one of the older clubs, and I had followed him in joining it—but I knew it quite well. I made use of my newly installed telephone to ring the club and ask the steward to tell Mr Potterton that I'd meet him there on Saturday. I had to admit to myself that this was much more convenient than going out to the call-box in the road.

I MEET MR POTTERTON 123

I thought so much about our forthcoming meeting that I almost forgot to be frightened. I continued automatically to take such precautions as I could—deliberately leaving a drawer open when I went out, and looking to see if it was shut when I came in—that sort of thing. But I was getting a bit bored with the whole performance, accepting philosophically that there wasn't much that one can do about the future, anyway.

From where I lived to the Corinthian at Salcombe was just over three miles by water. To get there by land meant going round by Kingsbridge and a road journey of nearly ten miles. Since I had no car I did most of my local travelling by boat. I enjoyed this, but it needed a close eye on the tide. The Salcombe or Kingsbridge estuary is not really the estuary of any major river, though it is supposed to have been so in prehistoric times. It is a series of deep inlets or "lakes", most of them draining a small creek, which become arms of the sea at high tide.* At low water most of them dry out, or nearly so, and if you don't watch your tide carefully you are liable to get stuck on the mud. On Saturday the tide served fairly well; I could get over to Salcombe comfortably at midday, but I shouldn't be able to get back later than midafternoon, because there wouldn't be enough water in Frogmore Creek. However, I didn't think that mattered much, for I reckoned that I could leave soon after lunch.

The wind was north-easterly, which gave me a fair run down the creek, and a pleasant sail across to Salcombe. The Corinthian has its own landing stage, and *Princess Charming* was already tied up there when I arrived. I made *Lisa* fast, and went into the club.

Mr Potterton must have seen me tying up, for he was at the door to greet me. He was most affable. "Mr Blair?" he

*See map, p. 12.

said. "Yes. I thought I recognised you. We *have* seen each other out sailing. How good your boat looks!"

"She's getting on for twenty," I said, "but she was built to last."

"Come into the bar and meet my crew," said Mr Potterton.

He introduced me to the girl I'd seen him sailing with when I brought *Lisa* round from Prawle Point the day after I'd found Edna Brown's body on the rocks. She was Anthea Newbury, the daughter of Sir Stancombe Newbury, who lived in a big house between Salcombe and Kingsbridge. She was a bright-eyed young woman in her middle twenties, wearing navy-blue slacks and a thick white sailing sweater. "I reckon Anthea is about the best crew in Devon," Potterton said.

"Have you been sailing together long?" I asked.

"No, this year only," replied Potterton. "We met in London—Anthea has a flat near Harrod's. It was one of those rather dull cocktail parties, and we suddenly discovered that we were both going down to Salcombe at the weekend. Wasn't that remarkable? Anthea had done a good deal of dinghy sailing but she'd sold her own boat last year, so she joined up with me. I call her the crew, but she's really joint-skipper."

The girl laughed. "Sounds nice in a bar, Angus," she said, "but it's not like that at sea! Put him at a tiller, Mr Blair, and he's like a brass-bound Cape Horner!"

I studied them both. He was not far off twice her age, but handsome in a powerful sort of way. His eyes, behind his gold-rimmed glasses, were a pale greenish-blue, curiously flecked with yellow. They were eyes, I thought, that would miss little. She was blonde, with almost platinum-coloured hair, and a complexion already hinting that she had used rather too much make-up from the age of fifteen or so. She was certainly vivacious, but I sensed a slight nervousness, or strain, behind the vivacity. I wondered just what their relations were. Well, it was not my business.

After a couple of drinks in the bar we went in to lunch. The girl was carrying a particularly large handbag in what looked like waterproofed sailcloth. As we sat down she showed it to me proudly. "What do you think of that for a bag?" she asked.

I remarked that it looked as if it would hold enough for a cruise.

"Angus gave it to me," she said. "It's his own design—a Utility Sailing Bag for women. You don't have our problems. You can't carry an ordinary handbag in a boat, and although you do have pockets in sailing clothes, you always forget to transfer things from your bag to a pocket. This bag holds everything you want, and it's waterproof, and looks nice as well. Angus is thinking of marketing it. I think lots of people would buy it."

"I don't know about the bag," said Potterton, "but I think I told you that specialised marketing is rather our line. What sort of furniture do you make?"

I told him that I specialised in high-backed cottage chairs and oak refectory tables, and that I was thinking of going in for dressers and linen-presses as well. "I like using old boat-building timbers when I can get them," I said. "There's not much around, but you can still come across the hulk of an old trading ketch sometimes, with bits of good wood still in her. I go all over the place looking for timber, and I've got a fair stock. You can pick up some decent wood now and then when an old house is being pulled down. You have to keep your eyes open, but I think I can get hold of enough of the sort of timber I want to keep going for the next few years, at least."

"Have you always been a cabinet maker?" Potterton asked.

"No, I spent a good few years in the Army," I said. "But

there seemed to be no future in it, so I came out. I think there *is* a future in my sort of furniture making."

"I'm quite sure there is," said Potterton. "Once we start advertising seriously your problem is going to be to meet orders. But we'll see about that. I like your project very much, and the thing to do will be to keep Blair Furniture rare and exclusive. I'm inclined to think that a rather subtle public relations campaign might be more effective than straight advertising. It will cost you a bit of money, but you'll get it back twenty times over. What have you got for display now?"

I said that I'd been making mostly for specific orders, but that I could manage various sets of tables and chairs. By early in the New Year I could have a couple of dressers and at least one press to add to the collection. So it might be better to wait till then.

"Yes, we must have a full collection before we launch out," he said. "When you're ready, let me know, and I'll send a really good photographer to take pictures. Or it might be better for you to send a set of furniture to London to get it photographed in a studio. What's your workshop like?"

"Not very impressive at the moment," I said. "But I'm negotiating for new premises and with any luck I shall be in them some time next year."

"Well, I think we'll have it done in London. You can get all sorts of effects in a studio that can't always be managed in a workshop. Let me know when you're ready to send, and I'll tell you where to send the stuff."

"He could be quite photogenic himself, if he'd let his hair grow a bit longer," said Anthea. "You know, the Artist-Craftsman at Home."

We all laughed.

I looked at my watch, and saw that it was just past two o'clock. To be sure of having water at Frogmore I'd have to leave as soon as I could. I explained this, thanked Potterton for having been so helpful, and said how happy I was to have met Miss Newbury. Potterton said, "But I'm in your debt, Mr Blair. This is just my line of business, and I think we may end up by doing quite a lot of business together."

The afternoon was clouding over, and I put on the oilskins that I'd left in the hall of the Club. As I was doing this, Potterton said, "I'll race you back to Frogmore, Mr Blair. I'll enjoy the sail, and as I've got to go back tomorrow I won't have another chance."

"Fine," I said, "but you won't be able to come all the way if you want to get back. We might just make Ham Point, but it would be safer if you turned round at the Salt Stone, before we enter the creek."

"O.K." said Potterton, "we'll see."

His own oilies were in the club, and as he went to get them he said to the girl. "Will you come, Anthea?"

"I'd love to, but I can't," she said. "We've got an elderly aunt coming to tea, and Daddy is picking me up by car at half-past two."

"So you won't get a sail at all," said Potterton.

"No, worse luck. And I've got to be at home all next week," she said.

"Why not have a sail with Blair?" Potterton suggested.

"Would you take me, Mr Blair?" she asked.

"Only too delighted," I said. "I haven't got a crew at all, and I'm a most gentle skipper."

"You really will be doing Anthea a kindness," said Potterton. "She gets stuck down here sometimes, and usually there's nobody about during the week. It would be a nice break for her."

So I arranged to pick her up at the club early on Monday afternoon. If we went for a decent sail I shouldn't be able to get back to Frogmore, but I could leave my boat on a mooring at Salcombe, and she promised to run me home by car. Potterton and I went to our boats.

*   *   *

I cast off first, and jilled around about a cable from the quay while he chatted for a minute or two with Anthea. Then he came out to join me, and we started as nearly as we could together. It was still blowing north-easterly, which meant that we were hard on the wind to get up harbour. There was quite a lot of wind, too, around Force Five, but it was a grand wind for the yawls, and they revelled in it. They were both Class boats and therefore pretty well identical, but *Princess Charming* was nearly new and my *Lisa* getting on in years, so that he probably had a slight advantage over me. But there was not much in it. On that early December afternoon there were few other boats about, and apart from moored yachts we had the water to ourselves. He kept fairly close to the Salcombe shore, but I stood over towards East Portlemouth, hoping to make a longer tack when I had to go about.

My manoeuvre paid off. He had a clear lead at first, but he hugged the shore a bit too finely, and had to make a series of short tacks to round Snapes Point without losing a lot of ground. I got a splendid slant when I put about, and was a good cable ahead of him when we passed the point.

From there to the Salt Stone off the entrance to Frogmore Creek was a hard slog of the best part of a mile. His sails were newer than mine, and this told. By the time we reached the entrance to the creek he had pretty well caught up with me.

The creek was losing water fast. It still looked all right, but I knew how shallow it was to each side of the narrow channel. Moreover, the creek runs more or less north–east—south–west. We were entering from the south–west, so that the wind was almost dead in our teeth. To beat up against it, with so little water, was going to be extremely tricky. I didn't think it could be done, and since I wanted to get home I decided to call off the race and ship my outboard.

We were almost neck-and-neck, about fifty yards apart, and I went over a little towards him to warn him to go back.

"I reckon it's a dead heat," I shouted. "There's not enough water for you to go on and get back. Thanks for the race. I'll be writing to you."

He acknowledged with a wave of his hand, and I busied myself with shipping my outboard and getting down the sails. The wind was dropping a little, and I thought that it would soon back, and the low clouds bring rain. The light from the short December day was going, and grey land was merging with grey water into a misty whole in which it was already hard to make out detail. I seemed utterly alone. I had been carried back a bit by wind and tide while fiddling with the outboard, and I was glad when the engine fired and I had steerage way again. I had just settled down to concentrating on the channel when I heard what I thought was another outboard. I looked round, startled. Good God, he was coming on! He was doing just what I had done, but he was still pulling at his outboard. *It hadn't fired yet!* Then, what had fired?

I have never known such utter, absolute panic as I experienced for a moment then. He was no more than twenty or thirty yards away. Why was he coming on? And had he fired a pistol at me? And if so, why? why? why?

Mercifully, the paralysis of panic didn't last long. His engine fired a second or two after I'd looked back, but I had a slight start because I was already under way. He had not waved when I looked back: he was huddled over his tiller, grimly determined, apparently, on just one thing—to catch up with me.

Well, I knew the creek better than he did. The first thing to do was to raise the plate to give myself more room for manoeuvre. He saw what I was doing, and at once did the same. I still had a lead of about twenty yards. I doubted whether I could shake him off, but I could give him a run for his money. Where the creek widens into what is called Frogmore Lake I swung hard to starboard.

This was a dangerous thing to do, because the lake is shallow, and almost all of it dries out. But the mudbanks vary in height, and at that state of the tide there were still runnels, or narrow channels, between the banks where we could go. In the misty half-light I was far from confident that I could stay in the runnels, but I had the advantage of knowing, at least roughly, where they were.

He swung round after me, but since he had not known that I was going to turn I gained perhaps another half-dozen yards. I held my course as long as I dared, and then turned through 90 degrees to port, praying that I should still find water to carry me between the high banks off Ham Point. I did, but he was a moment late in following, and I must have been carried over by the very last trickle of the ebb. I heard his outboard splutter as it hit the mud, and then there was silence. I looked back to see him pushing with his boathook, but I knew that it wouldn't be any good. He was stuck for several hours, until the flood brought back enough water to get him off. And he couldn't get ashore, because if he left his boat he would sink up to his neck in the soft mud.

I could not now make the head of the creek but I could still land about a mile short of the village. I made *Lisa* fast, and walked home.

I didn't think I had anything more to fear from Potterton that night. It would be pitch dark before he was afloat, and after his long sojourn on a mudbank all he'd want would be to get back to wherever he was staying for a hot bath and a meal. On Sunday morning I recovered *Lisa* and sailed back down the creek. Potterton had gone—I assumed that he had sailed back as soon as he could float last night. I didn't go on to Salcombe, where I might be seen, but turned the other way and sailed up to Kingsbridge, where I stood myself lunch at a hotel and spent the afternoon in a cinema: I thought I'd be out all day, in case Potterton should decide to call or telephone. I couldn't sail back, because the tide was wrong, so I left *Lisa* at Kingsbridge and walked home to Frogmore. A thread I'd put across the bottom of my front door broke as I opened the door, so the door had not been opened while I was away. Similar threads across the windows were unbroken. I inspected the cottage carefully, but all seemed to be well.

I was beginning to wonder if I'd imagined the whole chain of events on Saturday, but I knew that I had not. I had no evidence of any sort against Potterton, but I was quite sure that he had tried to kill me. He had fired at me when my back was turned, presumably with a pistol. Why had he not fired again? I could only guess. He had to look after his own boat. He had missed once, and in that light, and with the boats still some distance apart, he could not be sure of hitting me. And he did not want me to see him with a pistol: I might have got away (as I did), and had I seen him firing at me I might have gone straight to the police. Even if I could prove nothing, there would have been awkward inquiries.

But had he caught up with me ... I didn't like to think of what might have happened then. A shot from point-blank range, and maybe the pistol would have been put in my hand to suggest that I'd killed myself. Or he might just have left me, to be carried down with the tide and found shot wherever *Lisa* might fetch up. What was to connect him with me? The police might discover that I'd lunched with him at the club, and that we'd sailed off in company. But he'd have got back in good time, saying that he'd left me at the Salt Stone—with Miss Newbury to confirm that I'd recommended him to turn at the Salt Stone and not to enter the creek. His chances of getting away completely with my murder would be high.

But why? How was he mixed up with things? His advertising agency was genuine, if Sir Stancombe Newbury's daughter was his girl friend he apparently moved in reputable society. I decided to discuss it all with George, but I couldn't go to Exeter on Monday because I was committed to go sailing with Miss Newbury. And if I could talk to her first I might have more to tell George.

On Monday morning I telephoned Potterton at his office in London. A good deal to my relief he was there. Making myself sound as concerned as I could, I said that I'd been very much worried about him, and was exceedingly sorry that our pleasant sail had ended so badly. "There was nothing I could do on Saturday night," I said, "because I couldn't cross the mud to get to you. I went out to look for you as soon as it was light on Sunday but you'd gone. I didn't know where you were staying in Salcombe, or even if you might have driven back to London. I'm miserably unhappy about it all, and only hope you can forgive me for leading you into such a mess."

"It wasn't your fault," he said. "I should have taken your advice. I'm sorry that you should have been worried. I tried to phone you on Sunday, but I couldn't get any reply."

"No," I said, "you wouldn't have got a reply. I'm sorry about that too. After going out to look for you I was out most of the day. I had to go to Teignmouth to look at an old boat there, for her timbers."

"Any good?" he asked.

"No," I said. "She was sold a couple of hours before I got there."

"Bad luck! Well, no ill-feelings on my part, and I hope none on yours. We must have another go—I reckon I can beat you if I can stay off the putty. By the way, is it this afternoon you go out with Anthea?"

"I hope so," I said.

"What's the weather like?"

"Not bad. The wind's backed to the west."

"Well, give Anthea my love and have a good trip. I'm afraid it will be a month or so before I can get down again, but I'll let you know, and perhaps we can have a return match."

"And I hope you'll let me return your lunch," I said.

"I'll look forward to that. Good luck."

8

Breakdown

ANTHEA NEWBURY WAS waiting for me on the club jetty. She was well equipped, with oily smock and trousers, and was carrying her Women's Sailing Bag.

"You look very nice," I said.

"Thank you." She handed me her bag and climbed down into *Lisa*. "Where shall we go?"

"The wind's more or less in the west, and it looks like holding," I said. "I thought we might beat out round Bolt Head and have a good run home."

"That'll be fine. Shall I let go?"

"As soon as you're ready. But look, why don't you take the tiller and take her out? I'll cast off," I said.

She was obviously pleased at this, and came aft. I went forward to take in *Lisa*'s painter, and then took the jib sheets.

"I'll have to go about almost at once," she said as we moved from the jetty. "Ready about! Lee-oh." She put the helm down, *Lisa* moved briskly through the eye of the wind, and I hardened the sheet on the new tack. The girl freed the mainsail a little, and we sailed fast towards the harbour bar and the sea. She could certainly handle a boat.

"Your *Lisa* is a beautiful old boat," she said. "She goes like a dream."

"She was my father's boat. He loved her very much," I told her.

"And do you love her?"

"Yes. She's the only woman in my life now."

"That 'now' sounds as if she had a rival."

"Well, she did, once. But that was a long time ago."

Anthea saw that this was a line of conversation that I did not much want to pursue. She said nothing, but threw back her head and let the wind ruffle her hair.

We were approaching Splat Point, and the wooded slopes that climb up the cliffs overlooking Starhole Bay, and on to Bolt Head. They were winter trees now, but you could see the bones of the land the better for their bareness. It was a good skeleton, hard and spare, like the bone-structure that keeps a face beautiful in old age. There was a little sun to give sparkle to the sea, and I thought how clean and comforting it all was—the solid, secure land, the always-exciting sea, hinting at wonders round the next headland, fresh beauty, even new life, perhaps, beyond the horizon. In rough weather the bar at the entrance to Salcombe can be a nasty place, but it was quiet enough now, and *Lisa* danced over it.

"Do you live in London mostly, or at home with your father?" I asked.

She considered a bit before replying. Then she said, "That's not a very easy question to answer. I had a job as secretary to an MP but when my mother died about two years ago Daddy felt that I ought to come home and look after him. Have you ever met my father? No? Well, he's all right—a splendid person, really—but although he retired from the Army long ago he still feels that he's a brigadier in the sight of God, as you might say. When they made him a Deputy-Lieutenant for the County he was inclined to think that all the rest of us, including me, were lesser mortals. He's always slightly held it against me that I wasn't a son. There's no heir to the baronetcy, and he's always rather conscious that he's the last Sir Stancombe Newbury. I feel sorry for him quite often, but that doesn't make him easy to live with. All his friends are his own age, and there's nothing for me to do except to be around and sit opposite him at dinner. I stuck it for a year after mother died, and then the MP I'd been working for said he'd too much work for one secretary, and could I come up to London sometimes and help out part-time? Daddy didn't want me to, but mother left me a little money of my own, and I think Daddy knows that I'm not dependent on him, and that if he presses me too hard I'm quite capable of going off on my own. So I got this little flat in London—it's a bed-sitter really, but with a bathroom and a tiny kitchen—and I'm there quite a lot of the time. But I don't want to break with Daddy, and I come back fairly often."

She seemed extraordinarily frank. I began to like her very much.

"Do you see much of Angus Potterton?" I asked.

"It varies. Lately, quite a lot. He's an exciting sort of person, and he likes sailing with me. I think I like him, too."

I didn't follow up her "I think". It seemed to belong in the category of the "now" that I had not wanted to enlarge upon.

We had been sailing for about an hour and a half, but not very seriously; we had been talking and enjoying the sea rather than concentrating on any particular course. Anthea had left *Lisa* rather too free to beat up to Bolt Head, with the result that we were still well to the east of it. It didn't matter, but it was about time for turning back. "I've got a flask of hot tea in the locker," I said. "Let's have that and then turn round." I got out the tea and a couple of mugs, when Anthea said, "Will you take over for a bit, Peter"—we'd drifted into "Anthea" and "Peter" quite naturally, somehow—"I want to get something from my bag."

I took the helm, and she moved forward, and began rummaging in her big sailing bag. Then she looked up, with an extraordinary expression on her face, "Oh, my God," she said.

"What's up?" I asked.

She didn't answer, but searched her bag again. "It's not here," she said. "I never leave it behind, but I suppose I did somehow. Oh, God, oh God. Peter, can you give me a fix?"

All the niceness of her face had fallen away. She looked haggard and desperate, her eyes staring at me, but seeing Heaven knew what.

"I don't know what you mean," I said. "Have some tea."

She tossed the tea deliberately overboard, and hurled the mug into the bottom of the boat.

"Of course you do," she screamed at me. "I must have a fix, and I've left mine behind. I must have one now. You must give me one. You can't be a friend of Angus's and not have one."

"I still don't know what you mean," I said. "I have nothing to give you."

She began to scrabble in the locker, picking up everything she came upon and throwing it overboard in an intensity of rage—spare shackles, two more mugs, my Primus stove, all went over the side. Then she turned on me.

"What do you want?" she screamed. "You brought me out here! All I want from you is just one fix. You *must* have one! Do you want money? I'll give you a hundred pounds as soon as I get back."

I remained too startled and horrified to say anything. She gave a sort of leer, and began crawling towards me. "Do you want something else?" she said. "You can have it, if you like." She started tearing at her trousers. I leaned forward and slapped her face, hard.

She fell back on the floor-boards, and lay there, whimpering. Then she tried to pull herself together. "Oh God, Peter," she said. "I'm sorry, but I need a fix, I need it desperately. How soon can we get back?"

"I don't know," I said. "I'll do my best, but the tide's against us."

She raved at me again, cursing me, and the boat, and the sea, and everything else. When she had to pause for breath, she returned to whimpering.

"I can offer you a drink," I said. "You haven't thrown the whisky overboard, yet."

She said nothing. I keep a length of shockcord handy to hold the tiller temporarily when I have to go forward. I fixed this now, and went to the locker, where I had a bottle of whisky, mercifully in a fiddle right at the back. I don't drink much at sea, and carry the whisky mainly for emergencies. This was an emergency all right. The bottle was all but full.

Without letting go of it completely, I handed the bottle to her. She grasped it in both hands, and took a long swig. Then she spat, but she seemed a little quieter.

I had already made up my mind not to go back to Salcombe. It was imperative that she should not see anyone, or get hold of her drug, while she was in this state. Harsh as it might be, I had to get her to explain to the police what she had been saying to me. I decided to make for Dartmouth. It would take four or five hours, but the wind was fair, and we had been making leeway to the east—in the right direction—while Anthea had been raving. The problem would be to keep her quiet. If necessary I could knock her out and tie her up, but there didn't seem any immediate need for that. I still had my own tea-mug; I poured a generous helping of whisky into that, and handed it to her. She drank as greedily as before, and held out the mug to be re-filled. In about twenty minutes she consumed rather more than half a bottle of whisky, and she slumped in the bottom of the boat, beginning to be slightly comatose. I fed her another large drink, and she more or less passed out, lying on the floorboards, shivering. I had a couple of blankets in the forward locker, and I got those now, folding one to go under her head, and covering her with the other. Since I had no idea of what might be the combined effect of alcohol and deprivation of heroin, I fixed strong cord from thwart to thwart across her body, so that if she tried to get up in a frenzy, at least she couldn't jump overboard. She made no resistance, and I don't think she knew what was happening.

Lisa was on a broad reach, her best point of sailing, and I reckoned that we were making over four, and perhaps about five, knots. The outboard would not have taken her much faster, and I did not bother with it. I hadn't a great deal of petrol and I wanted to keep what I had for entering Dartmouth, when the engine might be needed.

It would soon be dark, but I wasn't worried because the Start Point light would tell me where I was, and I knew the entrance to Dartmouth well enough. We were utterly alone. No sound but some rather heavy breathing and an occasional whimper came from the girl. The usual comforting little noises came from *Lisa*, slight creaks as the wind-filled sails pulled at masts and rigging, and the chuckle of water at her forefoot. I had nothing to do but keep a light hand on her tiller. *Lisa* knew just what had to be done, and she was doing everything she could to help.

After about two hours Anthea stirred, and tried to sit up. I lifted her head, and managed to get a bit more whisky down her. She soon drifted off to sleep or drunken stupor again.

I didn't much like the idea, but I thought that I'd better have a look inside her bag. I put off doing so for some time, then I told myself that it was ridiculous to be squeamish about looking in the handbag of a woman whom I suspected of being in league with a murderer, and whom, in any case, I had succeeded in making drunk. It held the same sort of things that Sybil used to carry around with her, plus a small automatic pistol. I needed the torch from *Lisa*'s tool box to examine it. When I saw that it was a loaded Italian .28, with one round fired from the magazine, I considered it safer in my pocket, and did not return it to the bag.

We were off the mouth of the Dart by seven o'clock, and I shipped the outboard to motor up the river. There is a good quay at Dartmouth, and I went to the steps where the river steamers start from in summer. I had difficulty in rousing Anthea sufficiently to get her up the steps, and in the end I more or less carried her. I was thankful that it was dark.

It was not, however, late, and to my relief there was a taxi on the rank by the quay. I helped Anthea into it and asked the driver to take us to the police station. He was a little puzzled, because it was only a few blocks away, but I gave him a pound and asked him to hurry. He shrugged his shoulders, and in a minute or two we were there.

At the police station I had a remarkable stroke of luck—the constable on duty was the man who had navigated the fishing boat on our locket hunt. He was saying "Well, sir, this is a nice surprise..." when Anthea was suddenly and violently sick.

I said, "Please, can you get hold of Chief Superintendent Payne at his home, and ask him to come here straight away? It's very, very urgent. And can you lock up this young lady, and get someone to look after her until the chief superintendent comes?"

I was asking a lot, and he scratched his head unhappily.

"Arrest us both if you like," I said, "but for God's sake get hold of Chief Superintendent Payne."

"I don't know that I need arrest you, sir, but the young lady looks not far short of d. and i.—drunk and incapable, that is, sir," he said. "I'll ask the sergeant to ring up Exeter, and I'll try and get a woman PC for the young lady. Maybe we won't need to charge her."

"Chief Superintendent Payne will probably be at home," I

said. There was a message-pad on the counter. I wrote George's number on it and gave it to him.

"Thank you, sir," he said. "That will be a help. I won't be a minute."

He went through a door at the back of his office, but he did not shut it, and I heard him speaking to somebody. Then he returned.

"The sergeant would like a word with you, sir, when he's spoken to the chief superintendent," he said. "Meanwhile, we'd better take the young lady to lie down. Can you help me with her?"

Between us we half-carried Anthea along a short passage to a bare little room containing a bunk, a wooden chair, and nothing else. I suppose it was a cell. We put her on the bunk, and the constable considerately took off her shoes. It turned out a moment later that it was not quite the kind of consideration I thought. "If we take these away for the present, sir, she won't be able to get far even if she does try to run off. You see, I don't think I can lock her up—at least, not until the sergeant tells me to."

There were hurrying footsteps in the passage, and a policewoman came in. She was about Anthea's age. With a curious touch of formality the constable introduced us "Woman Police Constable Dorothy Jennings—Major Blair," he said.

"I'm to stay here until relieved," Miss Jennings said.

"That will be very good of you," I replied. "She's had—er —rather a lot to drink, and I think she's also rather ill. But don't get a doctor yet—unless you feel you have to. She ought not to see anyone until Chief Superintendent Payne comes."

Miss Jennings sat on the wooden chair, and the constable took me to the sergeant's office. The sergeant's manner showed that he'd been able to get hold of George. "The chief superintendent is on his way, sir," he said. "He says that we are to do everything we can for you. What would you like us to do?"

"Chiefly, to make sure that that young lady stays here, and that nobody apart from the police sees her, or knows about her until the chief superintendent gets here. I have reason to believe that she is a vital witness in a most important case. She's the daughter of Sir Stancombe Newbury, by the way."

The sergeant whistled slightly. "And you want us to lock her up?" he said.

"I think Sir Stancombe would be most grateful if you did," I told him.

Tactfully, the sergeant made no direct comment on this. "We'll look after her all right," he said.

Suddenly I was ravenously hungry. "And do you think you could get me something to eat?" I asked.

"That's easy," said the sergeant. "What would you like, sir? Would bacon and eggs do?"

I said they would do splendidly.

I felt vastly better for the meal. It was brought to me on a tray in the sergeant's office, and politely he let me eat without trying to make conversation. When I pushed the tray away, he smiled. "Better now, sir?" he asked.

"Much, thanks to you," I said. "It's been a day! Do you think we ought to have a look at Miss Newbury?"

"It might be as well," he said.

The cell was just as we'd left it. Miss Jennings got up when the sergeant came in. "She's been sick again," she said, "and she's very restless. She keeps on calling out for somebody that sounds like 'Angus'. And twice she said"—she got out her notebook—"'Your bloody work'—I'm sorry but that was the word she used—and 'You'll have to do it yourself'."

"You've done very well, Jennings," the sergeant complimented her. He looked at his watch. "The chief superintendent reckoned he could get here in about an hour and a half," he said. "That was over an hour ago, so he should be here soon."

We went back to the office, and George arrived about ten minutes later. I think I have never been so glad to see anyone.

"I've got a lot of things to tell you, George," I said.

"And I've got something to tell you. Where have you been? I've been trying to get you all evening. Manning was getting very worried about you. He said you'd told him you were going for a sail, but that you expected to be back around five."

"I'm sorry about that, but I couldn't get in touch with anybody because I was at sea."

The sergeant broke in. "There's no one in the inspector's room, sir," he said to George. "You could talk more comfortably in there." He took us to another office, and switched on an electric fire. "You won't want me, I expect," he added. "But if you press the bell on that desk, sir, I'll come at once."

As soon as he'd gone, George said: "There's been another message. It will be in *The Examiner* tomorrow. Pusey used your code and it worked. It gives a rendezvous for the 19th."

This was staggering news. I wondered how it would affect my story. "Today's the 11th, so that's Tuesday next week," I said.

"Yes, at least we've got a week," said George.

I scarcely knew where to begin, but I gave him a quick account of my adventure, of Potterton's extraordinary pursuit of me, and of Anthea Newbury's breakdown. "Of course, I can't be absolutely certain that he fired at me, though I think he did," I said. "And I found this in Anthea's bag." I gave him the pistol. "You will see that one round has been fired."

"We could arrest him, I suppose," George said, "though nothing would stick on your evidence. The pistol is suggestive, but at present it relates to the girl. If she hasn't got a firearms certificate there could be serious trouble for her, but I don't see how it would bring in him. In any case, there's only your word that you found it in her bag, and if she chose to deny all knowledge of it we might not get much forrader. The drugs are different. If she'd accuse him of supplying heroin, we could act on that. But will she?"

My mind was racing. "I don't think you should make any move against him, yet," I said. "Even if Anthea talks, and you can arrest him now, you may get him only on a comparatively minor charge. We *must* wait until next week, and see what happens at the rendezvous. If you can get him with smuggled heroin in a boat you'll have all the evidence you need. And with any luck you'll have evidence about the ship that brings it, and smash the whole ring.

"But Anthea is still vital. I suspect that he needs a girl to go with him in the dinghy, to make the outing look as innocent as possible. I imagine that he used to take Gwen Rosing until he decided to get rid of her. It's utterly and absolutely imperative that we get Anthea on our side. If he knows that she broke down like this in front of me he'll do nothing about next Tuesday. He'll probably change his system altogether, and you'll be back where you started."

"You're expecting a lot of the girl," George said.

"We can but try. Anyway, we must get her home at once—now, tonight. And we must talk to her father."

George got hold of the divisional police surgeon, Dr Hadfield, and without going into too much detail explained enough to impress him with the importance of the case. After examining Anthea, the doctor said, "She was completely passive, but she won't answer any questions, whether because she doesn't want to, or because she's still partly intoxicated, I don't know. As far as I can see she has a number of the marks of a heroin addict, but she's had a lot to drink, and some of the symptoms may be confused by alcohol."

"When she sobers up she'll be raving for more heroin," I said. "Can you do anything about that?"

"Well, I suppose I could give her a heroin injection, but she ought to have a long course of treatment. It's not impossible to cure an addiction, but the prognosis is not usually very hopeful. It depends mainly on whether she herself wants to be cured."

"Maybe she does. But can you keep her on her feet for the next week? Can you come with us now to take her home, and be there to do something when she sobers up?"

George seemed to feel that some explanation of my rather urgent questioning was needed. "Major Blair is a doctor's son," he said.

The doctor's reaction was a little surprising. "Not Dr Blair of Ashburton?" he asked.

"Yes, he was my father," I said.

"He was the finest man I've ever known," the doctor said. "He came to my rescue, once. It's a long story so I won't go into it, but he did something for me that very few men would have done. I shall be proud to do anything I can for his son. And, of course, for the police," he added to George.

It was getting on for midnight, and George felt that we ought to have a plan of campaign for bearding Sir Stancombe Newbury—even chief superintendents are conscious of the influence of deputy lieutenants of their own county. "I think you should ring him up before we leave here," I said. "Slightly stress your rank. Say that his daughter is in serious trouble, and that you are bringing her home in an ambulance. He'll almost certainly ask 'Has there been an accident?' If he does, I'd say 'No, sir, not exactly, but I cannot discuss it over the telephone. I'll explain fully when I come.'"

"How much do you think we ought to tell him?" George asked.

"We'll have to play it by ear, but my instinct is to tell him practically everything—about his daughter, at any rate. Look, George, you must do the ringing up, but when we get there will you let me do the talking? I've had the benefit of a long conversation with Anthea, and I think—mind you, I can only say I think—that I can get through the baronet to a decent sort of man inside. May I try?"

George laughed. "I'll have to play it by ear," he said. "But the partnership's worked all right so far."

The sergeant rang for an ambulance. Woman PC Jennings was a good sort, and volunteered to come to Newbury Hall with Anthea, and stay the night if necessary. The doctor and I left George alone in the inspector's office to do his telephoning. He came out in about five minutes. "I got through at once," he said. "The old boy was obviously worried because his daughter hadn't come home, and, if anything, he seemed relieved to know that she was on her way back, even in an ambulance. He's waiting up for us."

We travelled in an impressive little convoy. George, with a police driver in a big police car, led the way. The ambulance came next, and the doctor brought up the rear in his own car. The policewoman went with Anthea in the ambulance, I travelled with George.

Newbury Hall is the other side of Kingsbridge from Dartmouth, but at that time of night the roads were clear, and the journey didn't take long. On the way I said to George, "Major will go down all right with the brigadier-baronet, but do you think you can give me some sort of status? Do you think Pusey would accept a temporary attachment to the Home Office?"

"I daresay he would," George said.

Even in darkness, Newbury Hall was imposing. The long drive shone in the headlights white and clean of weeds, and a wide sweep of gravel brought us to the portico of the house. It seemed slightly improper that Sir Stancombe, in a green velvet smoking jacket, opened the great door to us himself.

The ambulance-driver and the policewoman helped Anthea up the steps, and the doctor went with them. "I'll take them up to Anthea's room," Sir Stancombe said. And then, to George and me, "Will you gentlemen wait in the library? It's the second door on the right."

The library was a magnificent room, a bright fire burned in a huge grate, and there were comfortable leather armchairs around the fire. Sir Stancombe clearly used the place as his sitting-room. Shelf after shelf of leather-bound books reached from floor to ceiling on three sides of the room. A mahogany step-ladder, for getting at the upper books, stood in one corner. Neither the ladder nor the books looked as if they were much used, but a big round table held a variety of country magazines that certainly looked read, and a regimental history of the 14th Gurkha Rifles, with a bookmark in it.

We had time to look about us, for it was a good quarter of an hour before Sir Stancombe returned. "It is late at night," he said. "May I offer you gentlemen anything in the way of refreshment?" George thanked him, but declined, and Sir Stancombe went on, "Your remarks on the telephone, chief superintendent, were exceedingly disturbing. May I ask you to enlighten me about what exactly brings you here, and what has happened to my daughter?"

Before answering his question, George said, "Permit me to introduce Major Blair." Sir Stancombe gave a little bow, and I added, "Temporarily attached for special duties to the Home Office." He nodded, and to my relief said nothing. I went on, "What I have to say, sir, will take a little time. For how long have you known that your daughter is a drug addict?"

He put his hand on a chair, and seemed suddenly a very old man. "I cannot say that I knew," he said, "but I have served in the East, I am a magistrate, and I am not unobservant. I have been gravely worried. I fear that what you say does not greatly surprise me. Unhappily, my daughter does not confide in me."

"Would you be prepared to help her if she did confide in you?" I asked.

His answer would have been melodramatic if it had not been so patently sincere. "I would give everything I possess for her to turn to me," he said.

He slumped into one of the big armchairs, and I continued, "We have evidence not only that Miss Newbury is herself an addict—you will appreciate that unauthorised possession of heroin is itself a serious offence—but that she has been associating with a man we believe to be a dangerous wholesaler of illicit drugs. We do not think, however, that she has yet become deeply implicated in these activities. He supplies her with heroin—whether he introduced her to it I do not know, but it seems probable—and because of her dependence on the drug she is very much in his power."

"You must do what you have come to do, and arrest her," said Sir Stancombe. "I am grateful for the consideration you have shown in telling me all this. May I ask that you let her spend the rest of the night here before you take her away? In the morning I will go to see my solicitor. I must do what I can for her, though I shall not attempt to mitigate her offence. I shall, of course, resign from the Bench."

I made a signal to George, who coughed slightly. "It is not in my power to promise your daughter immunity from prosecution, but I have no intention of charging her at present," he said. "There are many other things to be considered. Let Major Blair go on."

I waited for about a minute. Then I said as gently as I could, "Sir Stancombe, it is not for me to assess blame, but I am bound to say that I consider you largely responsible for the trouble she has got into."

George looked rather horror-struck, but the old man didn't react as might have been expected. Instead he murmured, in a sort of defeated way, "You may be right. I have not been much of a father to her. But the young nowadays are so—so —I don't know how to put it. What can I do?"

"You can snap out of feeling sorry for yourself," I said sharply. "You have a chance now, perhaps the last chance you ever will have, of winning back your daughter. She feels, rightly or wrongly, that you have very little use for her because she is not a son, that you regard her as nothing more than a decorative housekeeper. She herself, however, has very deep feelings for you. They are clouded now because of your relationship, but they are real. You can reawaken those feelings and, in doing so, help the course of justice. But it will require great courage, both in you and in your daughter."

He responded as I had hoped he would. "You can say much against us, but the Newburys have never lacked courage," he snapped.

"I didn't for a moment doubt it," I said. "Now this is what you have to do. We have reason to think that at some time in the next week or ten days the man I have been talking about will ask your daughter's assistance, probably in crewing for him in a dinghy. *She must do whatever he asks*. Between now and then, it is imperative that he should be given no indication that anything has happened to affect his relationship with your daughter—he must not know that either you, or the police, have any inkling of what is going on. This waiting is going to be hard on you both, particularly on Miss Newbury. She has another battle to fight—she must overcome her craving for heroin. We can give her medical help, but the only thing that can really cure her is her own will. You, I think, can stiffen her will, but make no mistake, it will be an uphill fight."

"I understand," said Sir Stancombe simply. He had changed beyond recognition from the defeated old man of a few minutes ago. Now that he had something to work for he had something to live for. There was nothing phony about his soldiering. He got up briskly. "I shall not ask you to compromise your intelligence system by telling me more than you wish, but I can help more effectively if you will explain your immediate plans," he said. "I take it you wish Anthea to stay here?"

"Yes," I said. "If, as I expect, the man concerned telephones her, I want her to speak to him in as normal and friendly a manner as she can. He will probably ring up later today, and as she may not be in any state to answer the telephone at present, I should like you to arrange that the call comes through to you. If it does, I should like you to say that Anthea is out, but that she has left a message, and repeat the message in these exact words—I'll write them down." He gave me a sheet of notepaper, and I wrote, "If Angus rings up tell him that I couldn't do all that he wanted, but that everything is all right. He's not to worry about anything, and I'm looking forward to another sail in *Princess Charming* soon." I read out what I'd written and gave Sir Stancombe the piece of paper, adding, "It's important that he should get that exact message, but of course, please add the normal polite things that you would say to an acquaintance of your daughter's.

"Now we'd better have a word with the doctor, and see how Anthea is. I must have a talk with her before we can make any more plans, but I don't suppose she'll be fit for much before this evening."

The doctor said that he'd given Anthea a fairly powerful

hypnotic, which should keep her sleeping at least until midday. He himself would come back then, and treat her as might be necessary. "She may wake with another craving for heroin, or it may be masked for a bit—one can't know," he said. She ought, he felt, to have a nurse, and if Sir Stancombe approved he would arrange this first thing in the morning. For the rest of tonight Policewoman Jennings had agreed to stay with her.

Sir Stancombe said that he would be grateful for anything the doctor could do, and asked, "Shall I get our own doctor to see her?"

The police surgeon looked at George, who said, "In the circumstances I think it would be wiser to keep things in our own hands at present. You may have every confidence in Dr Hadfield, and if he considers another opinion necessary at any stage he will at once arrange it."

Sir Stancombe accepted this without discussion, and George went on, "I have a woman detective officer in my own force with nursing training, and I'll arrange for her to relieve Police Constable Jennings—that will be better than bringing in a nurse from outside. I shall also arrange a police guard for Miss Newbury. He will be in plain clothes, of course, Sir Stancombe, and if you would permit him to stay in the house as a guest no suspicions will be aroused."

"Whatever you say," Sir Stancombe said.

"Good," said George. "Then I'll send him along after breakfast with Policewoman Agnes Greene to relieve Constable Jennings. I don't think that there is anything more that we can do tonight, Sir Stancombe, and we are all most grateful for the way that you have taken things. Major Blair will be coming back in the afternoon in the hope of seeing Miss Newbury. And now, I think, we should all try to get some sleep."

Sir Stancombe took us to the door, and we went off.

9

Anthea

"Where do you want to go?" George asked, as we drove away from Newbury Hall in the small hours.

"God knows," I said. "It's a bit out of your way to take me home, and in any case I've got to come back here later today. Drop me in Kingsbridge and I'll walk home. Do you think Sergeant Manning could send a car to bring me back here?"

"Why not come home with me now? I'll let you have a car for Newbury Hall, and the driver can wait for you."

"That's generous of you, George," I said.

"Not all that generous," he answered. "I've come to the conclusion that I ought to put a guard on you during the next week, and we're a bit short of manpower."

I had an idea. "It's tough on Mary to run the place like a boarding house," I said, "but I will come back with you for now. But I won't stay tonight. I'll ask young Simon Kirby to come down. I want to talk to that young man again, and if we have visitors he'll be useful to have around. He's a rowing man, and I'd say that he keeps himself pretty fit."

"O.K.," said George. "As long as you have somebody with you."

"He's got a car, too," I said. "So we'll save the ratepayers a police car as well as manpower."

George offered me breakfast when we got to his house, but after the bacon and eggs at Dartmouth police station I wasn't particularly hungry, and I wanted only to go to sleep. I went back to my old room, but before turning in I used George's telephone to send a telegram to Simon Kirby at St James's College. I didn't try to explain things in the telegram —I simply asked him to ring me at George's number at midday. George said that he'd turn in for a couple of hours himself, but that then he'd have to go to his office. He said he'd come home about 12.30 so that we could lunch together.

I was emotionally exhausted as well as tired, and it seemed that my head had scarcely touched the pillow before there was a knock on the door and Mary said that I was wanted on the phone. Young Kirby was scientifically punctual. I said, "It is asking rather a lot, but several things have happened and you may be able to help. Can you leave Cambridge now and drive to South Devon? And can you stay for at least a week?"

"Can do," he said simply. "Where do I go?"

"You come to my home," I said, and then I remembered that I might not be back from Newbury Hall when he arrived. So I told him to go to Kingsbridge police station and ask for Sergeant Manning. Manning had a key to the cottage, and having arranged things with Kirby I rang Kingsbridge. George had telephoned after the police sergeant had rung up from Dartmouth last night, so Manning knew that I hadn't let him down by not reporting my return. He said he'd be glad to help, that he'd give Kirby a meal and then pilot him to my house; if I wasn't there he'd look after him till I came.

George got in a few minutes later and we had a drink together. "I must say, Peter, there were times last night when I thought you'd have me reduced to the ranks," he remarked.

"You were marvellous," I said, "but you called it a partnership."

He laughed. "My dear boy, I don't know what the hell I'd have done without you," he said. "Anyway, I've got a piece of news which may please you. I'm a policeman, and I have to work by the rules. I took up with Pusey your somewhat unauthorised self-recruitment to his outfit, and I'm instructed to tell you that it's now official. He's been on to the Ministry of Defence, they've put you back on the strength and seconded you to him. You may even get some pay, sometime, though I doubt it. But your next of kin should get some sort of pension or gratuity if—er—if anything unpleasant happened."

I was greatly touched by this. "I'm not sure who is my next of kin," I said. "The ratepayers can sleep easy."

I asked George if the locket code message had appeared in *The Examiner*, and he showed me the paper. It was about halfway down the personal column.

Darling19123719710751130 For Ever

Using the Tuesday line from the locket figures this gave a position at 50.06 N 03.47 W. George had brought the Admiralty chart of the Channel from The Lizard to Straight Point, and the position turned out to be about six miles almost due south of Bolt Head.

"I suppose this is where we call in the Navy," George said.

"You suppose nothing of the sort," I put in quickly. "This is a job for me in *Lisa*, and nothing else. If you had a frigate, or a naval patrol boat, or a helicopter hanging around, the ship would proceed up Channel—I assume she'd be going up Channel—and nothing would happen at all. You could have her followed and searched, but most likely you wouldn't find anything—it would be dumped overboard, not with a buoy, but with a few hundredweight of iron. No, we've got to get the name of the ship, and actually see Potterton, or whoever it is—it may not be Potterton—pick up the stuff. You can have a fast patrol boat over the horizon if you like, and perhaps walkie-talkie radio to call her up, but the only chance of seeing what goes on is through long-range binoculars from another dinghy. I'll treat *Lisa*'s sails with soot—maybe the ratepayers will stand me some new ones when it's all over—and if it's the usual sort of grey day we'll be pretty well invisible in the swell, even half a mile away."

George considered this. "You may be right," he said, "but it needs thinking about. If you go, I'm going with you."

I said that we could go into details nearer the time. There was a week to wait, and a lot might happen in a week. I asked how the message had reached *The Examiner*. Was it from the Paris Office again?

"No," said George, "this time it was from Rome. But the paper doesn't have a Rome office on the scale of the Paris set-up. The message was placed through an Italian advertising agency. We've not been on to the Rome police, because we don't want to start inquiries yet that might arouse suspicions."

"It looks to me," I said, "as if Mr Potterton will be considerably irritated."

"How so?"

"Well, the fact that they used this method of communication, and the irregular appearance of the other messages, suggest that whoever is at the sending end doesn't know long in advance when he's going to have a consignment. Maybe there can be one only when a particular ship is coming to some port that takes her up Channel. I should imagine that Mr Potterton would prefer to stay out of Salcombe for a bit. This rather forces his hand. Given time to arrange things, I should think he'd try sailing from a different anchorage. But he hasn't had time."

I was back at Newbury Hall a bit after five o'clock. This time a butler opened the door, and said that Sir Stancombe was expecting me. He showed me into the library, and the old man took my hand with genuine emotion. "Anthea will see you," he said, "but first I want to thank you personally for what you said and did last night. I almost think that out of this horrible business may come a new life for both of us. Would you like to go up now?"

I said that I would, and I asked him if anyone had telephoned. "Yes," he said, "a Mr Angus Potterton rang up soon after ten this morning. I gave him your message, and did exactly as you said. It was all quite normal. I haven't told Anthea."

He took me up to Anthea's room, but did not come in with me. She was in bed, propped up with pillows, and looking very wan.

"Hullo," she said. "Daddy tells me that you are a big noise in the Government. I'm sorry I didn't give you your Major. Angus called you Mr Blair, and I didn't know."

"Peter Blair, cabinet maker, is completely accurate," I said.

"Well, I don't know. And I don't know whether to hate you or to love you for yesterday. I suppose it's better to be drunk than to be a murderess."

"I don't know what you mean," I said.

"Don't you? I thought you knew everything. Angus gave me a pistol and said I was to shoot you. He said that you were head of a drug-ring and screwing up the price of the heroin that he got for me. I was to say you'd tried to rape me, and everyone would believe me because I'm Daddy's daughter. I think I'd have done it, too, only I needed a fix first, because I've never shot anyone before. And that's where it all went wrong—I was so intent on remembering the pistol that I forgot the fix."

"Did it go wrong?" I asked. I was gambling heavily on two words—her "*I think* . . ." of yesterday.

"I don't know. Oh, Peter. I'm so muddled."

"Did you know that there was another girl?" I went on.

"Yes, a bit. At least, there was at first, but not lately. I thought perhaps he liked me best."

"He killed her," I said.

She lay back on the pillows, gazing at me, and saying nothing. There were dark shadows round her eyes, and the pupils seemed to withdraw deeply into her skull. At last, she said, "Peter, what do you want me to do?"

"Stop having anything to do with heroin," I said. She went on looking at me. "And then?" she asked.

"It's not so much a question of 'then'," I told her. "You're going to have a hellish battle first, but it's one you've got to win."

"I have stopped taking heroin," she said. She spoke matter-of-factly, as if it were a quite practical decision, like deciding to wear a blue pullover instead of a white one. She continued, "Daddy spent a long time with me today. We've both been bloody silly. Do you know one thing he said? He said, 'Anthea, you must often have thought that I regretted you not being a son. I want you to know that I'd rather have you than all the sons in the world.' It wasn't easy for him to say that, Peter—but I almost think he meant it. He said something else—you know he's inclined to talk like a Boy Scout sometimes—he said, 'You can do something for your country now more valuable than anything the Newburys have ever done.'"

"You can," I said.

"Yes, but what? He said that you would explain to me. I want you to explain."

"I'm not going to ask about your relations with Potterton," I said, "because that's all in the past. You made a shatteringly awful mistake. It was quite clever of him to tell you that I run a drug-ring, because that's precisely what he does —a vile, soul-destroying business. He needed a girl to help him in various ways, and he had one. But she fell in love with a thoroughly decent young man—in fact she became engaged to him—and wanted to pack up. So he killed her. The question now is, Whose side are you on?"

"On your side—and Daddy's," she said simply. "But if you know all this, why don't you arrest him?"

"Because there are a lot of other people involved—until yesterday, you were one of them. I scarcely know you, but I'm prepared to gamble that you were quite innocently involved. At least until yesterday—don't forget that yesterday you were contemplating murder. But I put that down to heroin rather than you. Others are not so innocently involved. We have to wait about a week. Then, with a bit of luck, we shall be able to break the whole gang—one of the really nastiest gangs that this country has ever suffered from."

"How do I come into it now? And why are you letting me off?" she asked.

I didn't answer at once. Then I said, "Your second question first. Only you know in your heart whether you have really done evil to other people, or just been a silly little fool to yourself. I *think* you've been a silly little fool. As for letting you off—you've got to work your own passage to a life that means anything. Now, how do you come into it? How far can I trust you?"

"I'm not a boy," she said, "and I can never be a baronet. But I'm still a Newbury. Lord, that's speaking like a Girl Guide!" She gave a thin little laugh.

"Okay," I said. "Potterton rang you up here this morning. I expected he would. I didn't know about his arrangement with you about me, but I thought there might have been some arrangement, and that he'd want to know what happened. I fixed up with your father that he should take the call if it came. I asked him to say that you were out, but that you'd left a message, saying, 'Tell Angus that I couldn't do all that he wanted, but that everything is all right, he's not to worry about anything and that I'm looking forward to another sail in *Princess Charming* soon.' Your father duly passed on the message, chatted politely with Potterton, and says that everything seemed normal.

"Now I expect that Potterton will want to see you soon, and I'm fairly sure that he'll want you to crew for him in *Princess Charming* one day early next week. What I want you to do is to act as if nothing whatever had happened. If he suggests a sail, go with him exactly as you have done before. It's asking a lot of you, but it's desperately important. After what I've told you, you can probably destroy me, and a lot of other people, if you like, or you can help to destroy him. It's up to you."

"I've already told you what I'm going to do," she said.

"Right. The first thing is to get yourself fit enough to go for a sail if he asks you. If he does ring you, about that, or anything else, tell your nurse, Miss Greene. She's a policewoman, by the way, though she's a proper nurse as well."

"Peter—you'll stay around, won't you?" she asked rather pathetically.

"I'll be around," I said, "but I don't want to come here again for a bit—I don't want anybody to start thinking. That's part of working your passage—you've got to go through this very much alone. But you're not really alone, you know."

"Yes, I know," she said. "Thank you, Peter. And anyway I've still got the gun he gave me."

"As a matter of fact, you haven't," I said. "I wasn't sure if you had a firearms certificate for it, and I thought it would be safer with me. We could get you another one, if necessary. But I don't think you'll need a gun."

She laughed—a proper little laugh this time, and the healthiest sound I'd heard her make. "So I'm going to be dished out of shooting anyone again," she said.

The police driver took me back to Frogmore, and I found no one in the cottage. But I'd not been in long before I heard two cars draw up, the first bringing Sergeant Manning, who'd been leading the way, the second Simon Kirby. They had both eaten, so I made some coffee, deciding that I'd cook something for myself later on. Manning didn't want to stay long, anyway, because he'd promised to help his daughter with some homework. I was glad to see him because I'd thought of something that might turn out to be important.

"Do you think," I asked, "that you could make a thorough search of a yawl lying to a mooring in Salcombe harbour?"

"Easy," he said. "But what do you expect to find in an open boat?"

"Not that, exactly. It's more a question of looking for traces of substances that may have lodged between the planking."

"Well, that would mean a bit more looking. But we could get someone down from the forensic lab. to help. How long can we have the boat?"

"That's part of the problem," I said. "It's just possible that someone keeps an eye on her from the shore, and therefore she mustn't be moved, and no one must be seen going on board."

He scratched his head. "I don't see how you can search a boat without going on her," he said. "And it would be better if we could bring the boat to Kingsbridge and have her out of the water. I don't quite see what we can do."

"Look," I said, "this boat lies to a mooring with a canvas cover on her. My boat belongs to precisely the same class, and has the same sort of cover. Could you take her out at night, substitute my boat, and replace her the next night? If you could do that there's a reasonable chance that no one would notice."

"We could probably do that all right. We'd need a good launch to tow your boat out, and tow the other way. Can I tell the harbour master so that he doesn't get excited if he notices anything?"

"I'm not sure. We'd better ask George Payne about that," I said. "Can you get on to him tonight? If he agrees, perhaps you could go over and see the harbour master tomorrow, and transfer the boats tomorrow night. If it's done at all, it must be done soon. I don't know what you tell the harbour master. Whatever it is, he must be told not to say a word to anybody."

"There was a jewel robbery not long ago at one of the big houses outside Salcombe. None of the stuff has so far been recovered. We could say that we have reason to believe that the thief used a moored boat as a temporary hiding place," Manning suggested.

"Excellent," I said. "But we must consult George Payne. He might want to come down."

When Manning had gone Kirby put his car in my yard, and I took him upstairs to his room. There are only two bedrooms in the cottage, so he didn't have much choice. But he liked the place, although it puzzled him a little. "I put you down as married with probably two children," he said. "Do you live here quite alone?"

"Yes, all by myself," I said. "I make furniture in a workshop at the back."

"Funny. I thought you were in the Army."

"Oh, that was a long time ago. You see, I *was* married once, but it didn't work out."

"Bad luck!"

"I don't know. These things happen."

I had a few bottles of beer in the cottage, so I gave him one and he stood chatting while I made myself some scrambled eggs. "I've accepted that Sheila is dead," he said.

"Yes. And now you're going to catch the man who killed her," I replied.

He took a long drink of beer, and I told him to help himself to another bottle.

"You know, Major—if you are a Major—you're a very odd bird," he said. "You pick me up out of the night and take me to some top brass at the Home Office. Then you bring me down here and I find you more or less giving orders to the local police. Now you tell me you're a furniture maker."

"Cabinet maker," I corrected.

"So what? What the hell are you?"

It was a question I found hard enough to answer to myself. "My name's Peter, by the way, and if we're going to be stuck together for a week, you'd better call me that. Gets over the Major difficulty, anyway," I said. "Look, Simon, you've been very good, and you've taken a lot on trust. I'm afraid I'm going to have to ask you to take a bit more. I'm a perfectly respectable ex-Army officer, at least"—I remembered George's conversation in the morning, though it seemed a hundred years away—"I was ex-, but at the moment I'm not so sure. Yes, I do make furniture—I'll show you my workshop in daylight, and I hope you'll admire it. But I'm much older than you are, old enough to be your father."

"Not quite."

"Well, nearly old enough to be your father. Life's an odd business, and you get caught up in all sorts of things you don't expect. You've been caught up in a great unhappiness. I can't give you back your Sheila, but I can, perhaps, help to secure justice for her. Will you leave it like that?"

"All right," he said. "It's a relief to be able to talk about it, anyway."

Soon after breakfast Manning telephoned. The chief superintendent had approved the boat expedition, he said, and would be coming down next day to have a look for himself. The tides weren't very convenient. The boat could be slipped at Salcombe easily enough, but the chief superintendent felt it would be better not to do anything actually at Salcombe. That meant taking her to Kingsbridge, and if it was to be done after dark it would have to be in the small hours of the morning, because of the tide. Could I get my boat up to Kingsbridge during the day, so that she could be towed down for the substitution without the police launch having to come up my creek in the dark? And could I go with them to show them which of the moored yawls to take? They'd send a car to collect me, and take me home.

I agreed to do whatever they wanted.

Taking *Lisa* up to Kingsbridge gave us something to do. Simon had done plenty of rowing, but not much sailing, and he was keen to learn. He had a good sense of boatmanship, and was soon handling the jib sheets well. At Kingsbridge we went to the police station to tell Manning where we'd left *Lisa*, had some lunch at a pub, and then walked home. When we got back to the cottage I said that if we were going to be up half the night we'd better try for a few hours' sleep.

The police car came just before midnight. The run to Kingsbridge took only a few minutes, and we found the police launch lying at the quay. She had already picked up *Lisa*, so we could start straight away. Simon went in the launch, but I said I'd go in *Lisa*. I didn't want her bumped or banged, and there is always some risk of over-running a tow. I was happier to be at *Lisa*'s tiller.

It was a dark night, but the police crew knew the estuary well, and in any case there was enough water for us not to have to worry overmuch about the twists and turns of the channel. The launch was in beautiful condition, her engine making no more than a slight hum.

I knew where *Princess Charming* was moored, because I'd

passed her quite often, but in the darkness it wasn't easy to be sure that we'd come to the right boat. In fact, the first moored yawl that I thought was *Princess Charming* turned out not to be. We didn't want to show lights, but I checked the name on her counter with a tiny torch, shielded by my hand.

The real *Princess Charming* lay about half a cable away. Her canvas cover fitted well over her counter. It was drawn tight, and it was some job to get enough of it lifted to be sure of her name. One of the policemen came into *Lisa* to hold her to the other yawl's counter while I fiddled with the cover. In the end I got it up, read the name, and all was well.

Then I went on board *Princess Charming*, cast off her mooring, and made her fast to the launch, afterwards bringing up *Lisa* and mooring her in *Princess Charming*'s place. This didn't take long, and we were soon on the way back. I stayed in *Princess Charming* to look after her at the end of the tow. She might be used by a wicked man, but that was no fault of hers. She was a beautiful boat, and I didn't want her scratched any more than I wanted *Lisa* hurt.

Back at Kingsbridge, the police had brought to the quay a lorry with a crane. With help from Simon and the police crew I unrigged *Princess Charming* and unstepped her masts. Then she was hauled out of the water by the crane, put on a flat lorry and driven to the yard at the police station. The main mast, with shrouds and halliards attached, was difficult to put on the lorry, so Simon and I carried it to the police station. A police car took us home, and we went to bed.

Simon and I were just sitting down to lunch, when George turned up. I offered him lunch, but he wouldn't stay, saying that he'd got to get back to Exeter as soon as possible. He looked serious. "I just came to tell you what we found," he said.

"What did you find?"

"A .28 cartridge case, and this." He handed me a plastic envelope, containing what looked like a small piece of cotton.

"What is it?" I asked.

He replied to Simon as much as to me. "It is a fibre from the dress that Edna Brown was wearing on the last day of her life," he said.

10

Waiting

WE ARRANGED TO restore the substituted boats that same night. *Princess Charming* had delivered her grim piece of evidence, and there was nothing more to be learned from her; the sooner she was back on her mooring, the better. We could have put her back in the water at Kingsbridge and re-rigged her in daylight, but we decided that it would be wiser to wait until it was dark. That meant another trip to Salcombe in the small hours, but it couldn't be helped; it was beginning to seem almost normal to miss sleep.

Before he went off, George asked me to come to Exeter after we'd dealt with the boats, for a conference with Pusey, who was coming down from London. He expected to get to Exeter around midday, and we'd meet in George's office after lunch. Simon was not invited to the conference, but George suggested that he should come to Exeter with me. Mary would look after him and show him round.

The night tow to Salcombe was a replica of the previous trip, but having restored *Princess Charming* to her mooring, I had *Lisa* towed to her own home in the creek. Simon and I came ashore there, and the police launch went back to Kingsbridge. It was not quite 0500. We gave ourselves some breakfast, and turned in for a few hours before Manning came to take us to Exeter.

George met me with news as soon as I got to his office. Policewoman Greene had telephoned from Newbury Hall to say that Potterton had rung up Anthea again. He said that he found himself rather unexpectedly able to take a couple of days off, and since the weather seemed fairly decent he'd like to put in another sail. He'd drive down overnight on Monday, sleeping at some convenient pub on the way, and aiming to get to Salcombe around 0800 on Tuesday morning. He would have to drive back to London on Tuesday night, so he'd like to make an early start for their sail on Tuesday morning. Could Anthea crew for him, and meet him at the Yacht Club not later than 0830? Anthea had said that she would.

I have never lost a feeling of slight wonder when navigation turns out right—when some predicted landfall comes into sight just about where and when expected. I had this feeling now. I had been expecting Potterton to put to sea on Tuesday morning—if our theorising was right, logically he had to. But it still seemed near-miraculous that our theorising *was* right.

"His rendezvous according to the locket-code works out at 1130. He's allowing himself plenty of time," I said. "He's got to get about six miles south of Bolt Head. Add on a couple of miles from his mooring—that makes about eight miles. He won't risk relying on the wind—he'll use his outboard, and it's a powerful one. It will give him a good five knots—he can count on four knots, even with a fair bit of chop against him. That leaves him about an hour in hand. He may need it, for the rendezvous time after a long voyage can't be more than approximate."

"The point," said George, "is what do *we* do?"

We couldn't pursue this at once, for Pusey came in, accompanied by Commander Seddon. Both congratulated me on my performance, although I couldn't help feeling that much of it had been due to luck. "You have given me a new respect for the late Mr Holmes's Baker Street Irregulars," Pusey said. "Though I hope George has told you that you are not exactly an irregular now—if you want to come off the irregular strength, that is. But we can discuss that some other time. We've got some hard planning to do now."

"Does Mr Pusey know about the latest Potterton call?" I asked.

"Yes," said George. "He got here just before lunch and we told him at once."

"I remain extremely puzzled by Mr Potterton," Pusey said. "We've gone into his life story ever since he left school —and it wasn't difficult, for there doesn't seem to be anything much in his life apart from being successful in the advertising business. He seems to have been a clever little boy, doing well at a Kent Grammar school. He missed national service because of poor eyesight—he seems always to have worn glasses. He didn't go to a university, but got a job as a copy-writer in an advertising agency. He was obviously good at it, because he soon got a better job with another agency, and by the time he was twenty-five he was a director of it. He did very well out of commercial TV— he was in on the ground floor, so to speak. He got a couple of really big accounts, and began to make quite a lot of money. Then his father died and left him around £20,000 —he was the only child. He used this to set up on his own account as Angus Potterton Associates. As far as we can make out he does a good steady business, though there seems endless coming and going among the 'Associates'. But I gather that this is pretty common in the advertising-public relations world. The firm is effectively his own, and 'Associates' come and go as they bring in, or lose, worth-while accounts.

"He has never married, though he seems to have had a fair number of casual relationships with girls who call themselves 'models'. He lives in a rather posh service flat, entertains clients to expensive meals, and collects stamps. He did some dinghy sailing at school, and belonged for a time to a sailing club on the Medway. But he gave that up when he began going to Salcombe. He seems to have no close friends, and to be comfortably off, if not rich. He's clearly got a slick facility for advertising, but for the rest he seems a colourless sort of chap. Advertising is rather a world on its own—the same people seem to go round and round from agency to agency, and back again. Everybody seems to know everybody else, and it's easy enough to pick up gossip, mostly malicious. But people seem to 'know of' Potterton rather than to know him at all well. There's not even much gossip about him, except for the various girls that he is supposed to have had in tow from time to time, and such relationships are considered so ordinary nowadays that they don't attract much notice. You've shown pretty conclusively that Potterton is deeply involved in this heroin-ring, but it's hard to see why, or what he gets out of it, except for money, which he doesn't appear to need."

"Have your researches into Knowledge Exchange produced anything?" I asked.

Seddon answered. "Yes," he said. "Those book-parcels are used for distributing heroin. Ninety-five per cent of them are innocent books, but the rest have tiny packets of heroin hidden in the padding of the book-envelopes. We didn't want to raise suspicions by delays in the post, so the first thing we did was to arrange with the Post Office for simple X-ray screening of batches of the parcels. That doesn't hold up mail long, though sometimes it's not particularly effective, for not everything is shown up by X-rays. But we had a bit of luck, for the distributors were using foil to make up the little heroin packets, and of course that showed at once on the screen.

"There's a lot that we still don't know. We don't know how the stuff is paid for, though we suspect that it's a system of credit-blackmail. There are some bad debts—there was a sad one on the list of heroin receivers from the second batch of parcels we examined. He was an undergraduate at Oxford, and he shot himself with a 12-bore the day his parcel was delivered. The Oxford police have the parcel, but we don't propose to say anything about it at the inquest—there's enough evidence of drug addiction and debt to explain the suicide. We've not yet got a search warrant for the Knowledge Exchange offices, so we don't know how extensive their lists are. But we've made an analysis of the addresses of parcels containing heroin, and it's a pitiful picture. Two undergraduates at different universities are suspected of stealing cheque-books. They've not yet been charged, but the local police say that they will be shortly. Another is believed to have made several thousand pounds by stealing rare medieval manuscripts. And these are merely a handful of cases from inspection of a few batches of parcels. When we can get hold of the full lists I expect a string of tragedies will come to light. It's a filthy business."

"Is there anything to connect Potterton with Knowledge Exchange?" I asked.

"Yes, there is, but not necessarily very directly," Seddon replied. "The Knowledge Exchange premises are in a small post-war office block, which apparently belongs to Potterton. He seems to have bought it five or six years ago as an investment. It's in the hands of an entirely reputable (at least, as far as we know) firm of estate agents."

"Careless of him, all the same," I said.

"Well, I don't know. Obviously he never expected to be found out. And when Knowledge Exchange was set up, it may have seemed just commercial common sense to keep office rent in the business. And even if Knowledge Exchange did come to grief, there'd be no particular reason to suspect the owner of an office block of being mixed up with it. Of course, we haven't examined the books yet, so I don't know, but I'd be surprised if there was anything to connect Potterton directly with Knowledge Exchange. The other tenants are all quite respectable—an insurance company, a solicitor, a firm of chartered accountants and an architect."

Pusey said, "What are we going to do on Tuesday?"

I'd been thinking about this ever since I'd read the message in *The Examiner*. Potterton's telephone call to Newbury Hall had now given us a fairly clear idea of the timing, but we still didn't have enough facts. "What does Miss Greene say about Miss Newbury?" I asked George. "Is she going to be fit enough to crew for him?"

"She herself says she is," George answered. "I suppose we can assume that she'll be there. The doctor has been seeing her every day, and he can't make her out."

"What does he say?"

"Well, by her own account she's been on heroin at least for several months. He has given her none, and he doesn't think that she's getting any from some secret supply of her own—she's pretty closely watched. She ought to be having severe withdrawal symptoms, but if she has, she doesn't show them. She walks about looking like a ghost, and spends a lot of time with her father. She makes no fuss about having Miss Greene in her room at night, she's polite to everybody, and asks for nothing."

"I'm not a doctor, but my father used occasionally to talk about drug-addiction," I said. "He reckoned that sometimes it can be cured by sheer willpower. I suppose most things can, if you come to that—willpower, or faith, or both. It's easier to call them miracles. Perhaps they are."

"Well, something seems to have happened to her. As I told you, the doctor hasn't got a view yet, but he discussed her at some length when I saw him yesterday. She's had a tremendous shock, from you, from learning that Potterton killed his last girl-friend. She also seems to be going through a tremendous emotional re-thinking about her father—and he about her, I daresay. All this may give her some extra dimension of willpower. Let's hope it keeps her going until Tuesday."

"Poor kid. Let's hope a bit more for her than that," I said.

Pusey coughed slightly. "Assuming that Potterton and Miss Newbury go off in his yawl at 0830 on Tuesday, what do *we* do?" he asked.

"The one thing we don't do is to escort them in a police launch," I said. "I think we've got to decide between two quite different lines of policy. If you think that there's enough evidence against Potterton now, let him come down to Salcombe on Tuesday morning, and arrest him on the yacht club quay. Get a search warrant for Knowledge Exchange, and hold for questioning everyone who turns up there on Tuesday before they've had a chance to hear about Potterton. We know—at least, we can assume—that some ship is going to pass six miles south of Bolt Head around 1130 that same morning. Whatever ship does turn up will be highly suspicious, to put it at its lowest. I don't know enough about international law to suggest what the Navy could do, but it could obviously do something. If it couldn't board the ship in mid-Channel, it could presumably shadow her to whatever port she's making for, and the police there could certainly go on board. I doubt if they'd find much evidence of heroin—the stuff would probably have been chucked overboard—but taken in conjunction with what we already know, and whatever might come to light from questioning Potterton and the Knowledge Exchange people, there might be a chance of breaking the gang. That's one policy. Let's discuss that first."

"We haven't got much hard evidence against Potterton," George said.

"The fibre from Edna Brown's dress found in his yawl will take some explaining," I put in.

"Yes, but where does it get us? All he has to do is to admit that he'd taken Edna Brown out in his boat. Why shouldn't he? She worked for him, there's no reason why they shouldn't have been in Salcombe together."

"He didn't say anything about it at the inquest."

"He wasn't asked," Pusey said. "We were so anxious not to bring out things at that inquest that I think we rather helped him there. A good lawyer could demolish the evidence about the dress fibre."

"As things stand, I doubt if we'd get a conviction," Seddon observed.

"What about his suggestion that Miss Newbury should kill me? At least I found his pistol in her bag," I said.

"You found *a* pistol in her bag," said Pusey. "She might say that he gave it to her, and tell her story in court. But would it stand up? The evidence of a drug-crazed girl? Again a good lawyer could almost certainly demolish it."

"Then we must think of our second policy," I said. "If he can be caught red-handed, seen to pick up a buoyed parcel of heroin in the Channel and arrested with it in his boat, then even the best of lawyers would have a job to get him off. It means taking a good deal of risk—worst of all, it means exposing Miss Newbury to a considerable risk. But I'm sure she's got the guts to face it. What I suggest is this:

"He must be allowed to leave Salcombe and make for his rendezvous without the slightest notice being taken of him. I'll sail Lisa out overnight, and lie up in the cove under Prawle Point. I'll leave again at first light, and get to the vicinity of the rendezvous well before him. I'll grey *Lisa*'s sails by dyeing them with soot, and in a normal Channel swell she'll be practically invisible at half a mile. I'll keep a sharp look-out, and the moment I see either a ship or Potterton's yawl, I'll be sure to keep hull down, but I'll try to see what he's up to through glasses. As soon as the ship has gone I'll follow him in. He'll probably go back to Salcombe, but it's just possible he'll make for Dartmouth, or somewhere else. Whatever he does, I'll follow him. It would be a good idea to have a Naval patrol boat a few miles off over the horizon —if you can get hold of a good walkie-talkie radio I could call her up as soon as he began to make for home. But I don't think she ought to come too near. It wouldn't take a moment to heave the heroin over the side, and I'm sure he'd do that if anything happened to frighten him. Then all the real evidence would be gone. I suggest that I take Simon with me in *Lisa*. George and a good posse of police can be a reception committee at Salcombe. Or, if I radio that he's making for somewhere else, they can go by road to meet him."

Nobody said anything for what seemed a long time. Then George said, "I don't like it."

"Neither do I," said Pusey. "But it's hard to think of anything better. There is risk, a lot of risk. There's risk to Miss Newbury—God knows what he'd do to her if he were scared. There's the risk of losing the evidence. But I think we're agreed that we've *got* to catch him with the heroin. And I don't see how we can do it without risk."

"What about using a helicopter to shadow them?" Seddon asked.

"I don't think it would work," I said. "You can't have a helicopter low enough to see anything without everybody's knowing that it's there. If I were on that ship, I wouldn't dream of throwing out a buoyed consignment of heroin with a helicopter hovering overhead. And I don't see Potterton picking up the stuff with a helicopter in the vicinity. No, I don't like my scheme any more than you do. I can see all the possible snags—but I can't think of anything else."

"As I told you when we discussed this briefly before, if you go out in your boat, I'm going with you," George said.

"If he did spot us, a yawl with three people in it would be much more suspicious than one with two," I answered. "I've more or less promised Simon that he can play a real part in bringing his Sheila's murderer to justice. This *is* his part, and

I don't want to let him down. The two of us would be a normal crew. There's no real reason why three people shouldn't go out in a yawl—or half a dozen—but I'm thinking of a man who'll be scared and suspicious of everything. I don't want him to see us at all, if I can help it. But if he did just happen to catch a glimpse of us, there's a slight chance that he might think us harmless—another dinghy out for a sail. With three up, he might begin to get worried. It's a question of limiting the risk."

"I can lie on the bloody floorboards if you like," George said.

"I think I'd be happier if George were with you," Pusey said. "Put it down to Home Office caution, if you like. But things may go wrong—badly wrong—and if there's a senior police officer on the spot at least it will help in drawing up the answer to a nasty Parliamentary question. No, Peter, you have a point and I can see your point of view. You and Simon may feel that you have a private war against Potterton, but this is more than a private war. I think I must rule that George accompanies the seagoing party."

"Okay," I said.

I revised my original plan of sailing *Lisa* out on Monday night, and arranged to take her out during Sunday night. She would be safe enough in the cove, and no one was likely to see her there, for the cliff path is not much used in winter. Not knowing what local allies—if any—Potterton might have, we decided to put another yawl on my mooring in the creek when I sailed out on Sunday night. One of the police at Kingsbridge had a yawl, and George said that he'd be able to borrow that.

Pusey had to get back to London, but Commander Seddon decided to stay on in Exeter. He and George arranged to go to Plymouth in the morning to discuss things with the Navy.

Mary brought Simon to police headquarters, to be driven

back to Frogmore with me. There was time for a drink with Pusey before he had to go for his train. He was exceptionally nice to Simon, and I blessed him for it. Simon, I feared, had probably had a rather tiresome day.

We had the weekend to get through before the first act of our own performance on Sunday night. I wanted to see Anthea, but I didn't want to be seen going to Newbury Hall. Simon, however, had his car, and there was no obvious reason to connect this car with me, so I thought that if we went after dark on Saturday there shouldn't be much risk. Using my newly-installed telephone I rang up Anthea on Saturday morning, and asked if I could call that evening. She seemed quite pleased, and said that she was looking forward to seeing me. She also said that her father wanted to speak to me. It turned out that Sir Stancombe wanted to ask me to stay to dinner. I told him about Simon, and he invited us both.

We filled in time on Saturday by going for a walk of nearly fifteen miles. The more I saw of Simon the more I liked him. He was becoming a little less withdrawn, and he began to talk of his own life. He had had a shattering experience, and he wasn't at all sure what he wanted to do. When he had thought that he and Sheila were about to be married, all seemed clear enough. He expected to get a Research Fellowship. That would give him rooms in college, but not accommodation for his wife. So he and Sheila had been looking at cottages in villages around Cambridge, and they thought they had found one they could afford in Balsham. They would make their home there while he worked in Cambridge —he thought that he'd probably have an academic career.

Sheila's disappearance, and—as he now accepted—her death, changed everything. He didn't want to stay in Cambridge, and he thought that he would withdraw his application for the Fellowship. As a highly qualified geologist he could probably get an overseas job with an oil company. He felt now that he would like to do this, and give up all thoughts of an academic life.

I didn't tell him that his Sheila had a notorious past as Gwen Rosing. He was bound to learn that sooner or later, and it would be further misery for him. But the more philosophical he could be now, the better prepared he would be to meet that blow when it came. In the end he might even come to feel that death had spared Sheila from what inevitably would have been a difficult life for both of them. I thought that a few years abroad in the tough physical conditions, perhaps, of Alaska or the Arabian desert, would be the best therapy for him. But I told him not to be too certain of wanting to abandon all hopes of an academic future. "I think you'd be wise to leave Cambridge for a time if you can," I said, "but you are likely to have a lot of life left, and things may look quite different in ten—even in five—years' time. You will be a better Professor of Geology for putting in a good spell of fieldwork. And not only a better Professor— you'll be a much bigger person. There's a kind of academic in-breeding that makes Fellows, Lecturers and Professors only two-dimensional people. I'm an ex-soldier and I've never been to a university, but I've always felt that I'd love to have a university job of some sort after an active life—even a bursar's job, which is the only sort that I could ever hope for. You've got a chance of the real thing—years of hard activity in the field, and then academic distillation of all your experience. Don't mess it up. Go abroad now, certainly—but keep in touch with Cambridge. You know what you can do. Write papers in the right places, maybe produce a new text book on some aspect of field geology. Keep your options open."

I don't know whether this helped him much, but at least it directed his thinking to the future, and away from the past.

*   *   *

Anthea must have had a word with her father, for we'd hardly made our entrance and been offered a preliminary sherry before Sir Stancombe took off Simon to see his gun room.

Anthea poured me a large whisky from the bottle on Sir Stancombe's cocktail cabinet. "It's my turn now," she said. "But at least I'm not going to make you drunk."

I ignored this. "I think you are being very brave," I said.

"Why? What is going to happen?"

"I don't know," I said, truthfully. Then I thought of something, and added, "You are going to have something like four hours with Mr Potterton. If he offers you some heroin to break the monotony—don't."

"I told you that I've given up heroin," she said.

I put down my whisky glass and took both her hands. "Sir Anthea Newbury, Bart., after all," I said.

"Except that your bloody male-chauvinist world won't have it." But she didn't snatch her hands away.

When Sir Stancombe and Simon came back, I gathered that Simon had already accepted an invitation to shoot over the Newbury estate. We talked of this, and that, and had a very pleasant dinner.

11

At Sea

ON SUNDAY MORNING Simon and I stored *Lisa*. Her sails had been soaking in a bath of soot and water, the soot extracted from my chimney. They emerged a horrible, muddy grey, and we hung them on a line to dry behind the cottage. We loaded twelve gallons of petrol in three four-gallon jerricans—enough to take us sixty miles or so. We also stocked up with food, and I replaced the bottle of whisky which had been poured into Anthea. Then we went for another long walk and, since we were going to be up for a good deal of the night, turned in for a few hours after an early supper. I didn't sleep, and went down at once when I heard a knock on the door. It was a policeman, who had been one of the crew on the towing-launch. "My boat's in the creek, sir," he said. "I'll put her on your mooring as soon as you're away."

I collected Simon, and the three of us walked to the creek. It was not much of a night, dark and starless, and with a stinging wind from the east. But I welcomed the easterly, for it would take us nicely through the Salcombe moorings and out to sea, without requiring any noise from the engine. I was very pleased with *Lisa*'s muddy sails; admittedly, it was dark, but white sails normally show up well at night. Now at a few yards they were invisible.

The tide was just past the flood, and with the easterly wind we had a fine reach down the creek and through Salcombe harbour. We passed within half a cable of *Princess Charming*, peacefully lying to her mooring. I wondered in what circumstances we would meet her next.

Beyond the bar we had to turn to the east, which put the wind dead on *Lisa*'s nose. We hardened in the sheets for a stiff beat up the coast to the cove. There was quite a chop, and we took a good deal of spray on board, but there seemed no point in using the engine, and we didn't have far to go. We were carrying no lights, so I stayed well offshore. There wasn't much chance of meeting anything, but I didn't want to take risks of any sort.

It was impossible to make out any details of the coast, but I knew how to find Prawle Point. We stood out to sea until we picked up the flash from the lighthouse at Start Point, and when I judged that we had come about far enough we stood inshore until the light disappeared. The light is masked by the headland of Prawle Point, so when it disappears you are in line with the two headlands of Prawle and Start Point. By keeping the light appearing and disappearing I reckoned that we were roughly on the right line, and we stood in cautiously towards land. The rock where I had found Gwen Rosing's body marked the entrance to the cove. It was all but covered now, but with the lop a fair amount of spray was thrown up from it, and we were able to pick it up before getting dangerously close. After that it was plain sailing. I lifted the plate and put *Lisa* gently on the beach. We had brought hot coffee in a flask, and we stayed in *Lisa* while we drank it. With the falling tide it wasn't long before we could step ashore dry-shod. We ran out the anchor for when the tide came back, made *Lisa* snug, and set off up the cliff to walk home.

The day dragged horribly. There was nothing we could do now but wait for Tuesday morning. George was coming to the cottage on Monday evening to have a meal and get some sleep before setting off with us to the cove in the small hours.

I wanted to be away by 0730, and that meant getting there well beforehand to keep *Lisa* afloat on the falling tide. I spent a lot of time poring over the chart, though the distances were so short that there was no real navigational problem. From the cove to the rendezvous six miles south of Bolt Head was a perfectly straightforward sail, considerably shorter than the eight miles or so that Potterton would have to cover from Salcombe. But to get to the rendezvous we had to cross the entrance to Salcombe, and I wanted to be well away before there was any possibility of meeting *Princess Charming* coming out.

The problem was timing, not navigation. Assuming that Potterton left Salcombe at 0830—the only time we had to work on—he could be at the rendezvous from about 10.15 onwards—a little earlier if conditions were good and he motored hard, a bit later if he had wind and swell against him. I regarded from 1000 to 1100 as zero hour for him, from 1100 onwards as the critical time for the appearance of whatever ship he was due to meet. The nominal time of meeting was 1130, but that was in a message originating—apparently—in Rome at least nine days beforehand, possibly some days more. With wind, weather and sea unguessable so long in advance, no such rendezvous could be kept with split-second accuracy, though a big, powerful ship could expect to run to time pretty well. But we had no idea what sort of ship she was; her age, size, speed, whether she was loaded or light, were all unknown quantities. So were her points of departure and destination. Rome suggested that she would be coming from the Mediterranean, but there was no certainty of this. There could be an infinity of reasons for sending a message via Rome.

We could not even know whether the ship would be coming into the Channel from the Atlantic, or down-Channel from some French, Dutch, German or Baltic port. Since her consignment of heroin almost certainly came from the East, it was reasonable to suppose that she would be coming up-Channel. That meant that she had to traverse the Atlantic north of the Azores, and cross the mouth of the Bay of Biscay. The Navy had given us weather reports for the area for every day over the past week. There had been nothing sensational, the usual North Atlantic mix, which would not much affect a big ship, though strong easterly winds might delay a small vessel by some hours.

Our problem was to get near enough to the rendezvous to see, and to try not to be seen. Given the luck of a grey day, I reckoned that we should be safe enough two miles away, and reasonably safe up to a mile. But that cut both ways. What hides a small boat at sea is the swell, but swell equally interferes with vision from a small boat. If we kept too far off we should see nothing at all. We *had* to get near enough to see, which meant that we could also be seen. I hoped, however, that Potterton's attention would be fixed on picking up whatever was thrown from the ship, and that the ship's attention would be focused on Potterton, so that nobody would be particularly looking out for us.

That raised another problem: should we keep inshore of the rendezvous or stay to seaward of it? If we were spotted to seaward we should probably attract less attention, but if we wanted to get back quickly we should have farther to go. Moreover, an ocean-going ship would not want to get too close to the land, and if there were any hanging about she herself would keep to seaward. There are a fair number of wrecks on the Channel bed off the South Devon coast, and although they would not worry a shallow-draughted vessel, a big ship would be anxious to steer clear of them. Inshore of the rendezvous and a few miles to the north-west the chart showed a patch of shallows, easily located by cross bearings on Bolt Head and Bolt Tail, the next prominent headland from Bolt Head. I decided to keep between the shallows and the rendezvous. No big ship would approach from inshore of the shallows, which limited our arc of look-out to the south and west. It was, of course, just possible that the ship would be coming down-Channel from the east, but I did not think this likely. In any case, she would keep away from the shallows, and so keep away from us.

George telephoned to say that he would be late, and that he would have a meal before he came. It was nearly ten o'clock before he turned up. "It's been a hell of a day," he said. "The Navy seems to think it's going to intercept a hostile fleet. If they had a battleship, I'm sure they'd want to use her. As it is they're providing a submarine and a couple of frigates. Very nice of them, really. I hope to goodness they don't get in the way."

The submarine was the Navy's own suggestion, and it seemed a good idea. The chart shows most of this part of the Channel as a submarine exercise area, so there would be nothing out of the way in seeing a submarine—if she did happen to be seen. But the Navy did not intend her to be seen. She was to stay submerged at nearly the limit of periscope vision from the rendezvous. Her task was to see what she could, and then to make certain of identifying the ship. She would then shadow the ship to whatever port she was making for, signalling course and speed as she went along. As soon as a port of destination seemed probable the Navy would get in touch with the authorities, who would arrange a suitable reception for her. The police and appropriate Admiralties in the various countries to which she might be making had already been alerted.

The frigates were to keep at least ten miles from the rendezvous, one to the west, the other to the east. The Navy had lent George three high-grade walkie-talkie radios, which were supposed to have sufficient range to call them up. If we had any trouble in making contact with one or other of the frigates, we were to call up the coastguard, who would get in touch with Plymouth for a Naval wireless signal to be sent out. It all seemed highly efficient. The thought of *Lisa* as the key vessel in this Naval task force was rather splendid. It seemed a pity that in all the high-powered Naval activity going on nobody had thought of giving her a warrant to wear the White Ensign.

We went as far as the coastguard station in George's car, and it was as well, for we had a lot to carry: three of the Navy's walkie-talkie sets, a big picnic basket of food, binoculars, oilskins and heavy pullovers. I was thankful that I'd taken on petrol before leaving the creek. It was quite a job to get all the kit down the cliff path in the dark, but we managed it without breaking ourselves or anything else. *Lisa* was afloat, but on a falling tide she would not be afloat for long. George and Simon had only ankle-length rubber boots, so they went on board in shallow water. I was wearing sea-boots, and when the others were on board I waded in to push her off. Then I poled her into deeper water where she could safely stay afloat, and we relaxed at anchor for a bit.

It was too early to start. We could expect several hours of hanging about between Bolt Head and Bolt Tail, and we didn't want to be out there for longer than we had to be. It was not much of a morning. The persistent easterly was still blowing, around Force four, which kept the weather dry, but also cold. It would give us an easy run to Bolt Head, but we should have to beat back if the wind stayed where it was. I expected Potterton to use his outboard—he had no reason not to, for his whole dinghy-smuggling scheme depended on being seen, and, if necessary, heard, to be out openly. Since we were going to try to shadow him, I didn't want to use the outboard at all. We carried plenty of fuel for possible emergencies, but *Lisa*'s job was to sail.

We were all restless, and although I reckoned that we didn't need to start before 0730, we were away soon after

0700. The brisk easterly took us rapidly across the entrance to Salcombe, and well before 0800 we were safely out of the way. If he left at 0830 I expected him to cross the bar around 0900, but there seemed no point in trying to watch him come out. It would simply add to the risk of being spotted, and contribute nothing to our knowledge—if he were going to keep his rendezvous he had to come out. If for some reason he didn't appear, then there would be a new situation and all our plans would have to be changed.

I'd marked the rendezvous on the chart, and plotted compass bearings on every landmark in the vicinity—Prawle Point, Bolt Head, Gregory Rocks and the Ham Stone, and the radio masts on Bolberry Down, between Bolt Head and Bolt Tail. I'd pored over them so much that I knew them all by heart. I had a good hand-bearing compass, and I'd checked for deviation and error the day before. Admittedly, this was somewhat rough, but taking compass bearings from a small boat in anything of a chop is at best a rough-and-ready process. I was confident enough that I should know where we were.

With time in hand, I thought that our best course would be to make for the rendezvous before there was any chance of anybody else's getting there. We could get the feel of the place and the sense of distance off the coast before we stood away towards the shallows where we were going to try to hide.

The rendezvous was almost due south of Bolt Head, so we had a fair reaching wind, and ran off the six miles in little more than an hour. We were there before 0900, when Potterton, I thought, would still be coming out of Salcombe. There was nothing to see. There was a fair swell, but not much broken water. Westward, however, towards the shallows, waves were breaking a bit, and I felt that this was all to the good. We ran a couple of miles to the west, hove to, and settled down to wait.

BOLT HEAD TO PLYMOUTH

0 1 2 3 4 5 Miles (approx)

N ←

Plymouth
Breakwater
Plymouth Sound
RIVER YEALM
Bigbury Bay
RIVER ERME
RIVER AVON
Bolt Tail
BOLBERRY DOWN
RADIO MASTS
HAM STONE
GREGORY ROCKS
Bolt Head

ENGLISH CHANNEL

SHALLOWS →

One of the virtues of a yawl is that she will normally heave to well, but we couldn't stay hove to for long at a stretch. There was the tidal stream to reckon with, and the leeway we were bound to make: we couldn't afford to drift too far from the rendezvous, and in any case we were too close to the shore to sit back and do nothing. I kept a close check on our position by taking bearings every few minutes. We hadn't yet had breakfast, and I allowed us long enough hove-to to eat our bacon sandwiches and drink a cup of coffee. Then I let the sails draw again, and for the next hour or so we went through the tedious process that is known as "darning the water"—a self explanatory phrase, descriptive of sailing up and down over a cable or so, like making darning stitches on a patch of water.

A few minutes after 1030 Simon, who had superb eyesight, said, "I think I can see a boat." He took the glasses, and went on, "Yes, it's them all right. A yawl with blue sails." A moment later he lost sight of them as we sank into the hollow of a swell. When we climbed again I was able to see them myself. We each had glasses, and I got mine focused just before we lost our target in the swell again. It was certainly *Princess Charming*, but she was a long way off. Even with glasses, it was hard to make out any detail.

"We've got to get a bit closer," I said, "but we've plenty of time in hand, and we won't go nearer until we've seen what he intends to do. He's got to kill time, too. We're well downwind of the rendezvous, but that doesn't matter to us because we only want to see what happens. He's got to be there, to pick up whatever is thrown from the ship. He'll almost certainly stay up-wind, to be sure of getting there quickly when he wants to. From our point of view that's all to the good. We'll beat back slowly towards him, just keeping him in sight until there's some sign of a ship."

Keeping Potterton's yawl in sight, however, was easier said than done. The day was deteriorating, the wind was now gusting a good Force five, and the sea was becoming much more broken. He was as liable to vanish in a swell as we were. The best we could hope for was an occasional glimpse of him. To keep up-wind of the rendezvous, however, he also was compelled to beat, and since he didn't want to get too far away, he stayed well reefed down, and made no effort to sail fast.

As I expected, he stayed upwind of the rendezvous, and worked his way slowly to seaward of it. The ship would come from seaward, and once they had seen each other it did not matter where they were. I moved inshore a little and made short tacks up the coast, gradually gaining on him laterally, but not attempting to follow him out to sea.

Time passed quickly now. George and Simon concentrated on keeping Potterton in sight, I had my hands full in looking after *Lisa*. Then George glanced at his watch, and said, "It's 1145. Time something started happening."

But nothing happened. From time to time we would catch a glimpse of *Princess Charming*, now not much more than a mile away, lying hard over as Potterton slowly fought his way to windward. For the rest, the whole seascape was empty. The horizon was closing in as the weather worsened. The world seemed to hold nothing but Potterton's yawl and ourselves.

Noon came and went. At 1207 Simon said, "There's something on the horizon—coming up from the south-west." For a moment neither George nor I could make out anything, and then, almost together, we saw a ship. She was coming up quite fast. A moment later it was evident that Potterton had seen her, too, for he altered course towards her.

We followed, on a parallel course, a little over half a mile to the west. George said, "Simon, you watch the yawl. I'll watch the ship." Simon nodded, but said nothing. I needed both hands for *Lisa* and so couldn't use glasses, but we were all closing fairly rapidly now and when we rose to a swell I could see both *Princess Charming* and the ship.

The ship was a biggish oil tanker, with a bridge deck and short funnel astern, and a huge, whale-like expanse of tank-deck forward. George had his glasses on her. "I can make out her name," he said. "It's *Mount* something—yes, *Mount Vernon*. She'll belong to the big Mountain Line, I suppose." A minute later he gasped excitedly. "Something's gone overboard."

With naked eyesight I had seen it, too. I couldn't make out what it was, but something had been thrown into the sea from the ship. She didn't slow down, but altered course slightly away from the coast and steamed on. In what seemed an incredibly short time she was again hull down on the horizon, going east.

In an agony of concentration, George kept his glasses on whatever had been thrown from the ship. "I can see it now —no, I can't—yes, I can," he said. "It's floating, and it's got a flag, or something, on a short staff."

Simon, who had kept his own steadfastly on *Princess Charming*, put in, "And our friend is going over to pick it up."

The tanker had thrown its package overboard a little to the west of the actual rendezvous position, that is, on our side of it. This, and the excitement of watching, had brought us a good deal nearer to *Princess Charming* than we should have been. We could now see everything clearly. Anthea was at the helm, handling the yawl, in that stiff breeze and broken sea, extremely well. Potterton had gone forward, and was leaning over the starboard bow, ready to grab the buoyed package as they came up to it. Anthea brought the boat close in, and he reached out and caught the stuff. He had a struggle to get the package on board. It was obviously fairly heavy, and with his body hanging over the gunwale he had no purchase for the lift. But he was intelligent—or he had

had a lot of practice. He waited until a wave lifted the weight, and then swung buoy and package inboard. Then he straightened up and looked straight at us. I waved to him. He did not wave back.

Being upwind of us he came towards us very fast. He said something to Anthea, and for a moment I thought he intended to ram us. Then what he was going to do became all too clear. Steadying himself against *Princess Charming*'s shroud with his left hand he held a pistol in his right, and fired. The bullet went clean through *Lisa*'s planking, between Simon and me, fortunately well above the waterline.

"That's no twenty-eight," said George. "He's got a big forty-five. But I've got a pistol, too." Kneeling on the floorboards, George fired back. His shot tore a small hole in *Princess Charming*'s mainsail, but went well wide of Potterton.

He had the advantage of being upwind. When he started coming towards us I was hard on the wind, making an inshore tack. That meant that we had to cross his bows, giving him a broad target, while to us he was still head on. He raised his arm to fire again, aiming, as far as I could see, at me.

"That bloody girl's changed sides," George said. "She's steering while he shoots. Peter, can you swing us round a bit? I can't see the bastard properly."

Expecting to be shot at any moment I eased the sheets to bear away, when George cried out, "No she hasn't!" Anthea had wrenched the heavy mahogany tiller from its socket in the rudder stock, and I looked up just in time to see her crash it down with all her strength on Potterton's head. Several things then happened at once. He fired as he fell, the bullet going harmlessly skywards. With her rudder suddenly free, *Princess Charming* gybed, lost way, and sagged off into the wind.

"Stand by to board!" I said, and brought *Lisa* alongside *Princess Charming*. George and Simon grabbed her, and were over in a split second. Potterton was lying on the floor-boards, just beginning to stir. Before he had a chance to reach his pistol both George and Simon were on him. Simon held his legs while George turned him over so that he lay face downward. George then brought his arms across his back and put handcuffs on his wrists, so that they were held behind his back. Anthea had slumped down in the cockpit; she had fainted. I couldn't leave *Lisa*, but *Princess Charming* would soon be in a bad way. "Get the mainsail off her," I yelled.

Leaving George to deal with Potterton Simon jumped for the halliards and brought down the big sail before the swinging boom knocked anybody out. With the mainsail off her, *Princess Charming* was happier. I dropped *Lisa*'s main, too, and Simon made fast a line from *Lisa* to a cleat on *Princess Charming*'s counter. Then I dropped *Lisa*'s jib, so that she fell away astern of the other yawl. "Get the tiller back," I called to Simon, and when he'd done this I hauled up *Lisa* and went on board. I backed *Princess Charming*'s jib, and set the mizzen, so that she was more or less hove-to. The boats drifted slowly to leeward, *Lisa* lying off, a few yards astern.

I could now give some attention to Anthea. She was crumpled in a small forlorn heap in the stern, but she was coming to. The sea was kicking up and the yawl, with no forward way to steady her, was being flung about in an uneasy, jerky fashion. I got an arm round Anthea's shoulders to lift her back on to the seat, when she was horribly sick. I soaked my handkerchief in seawater and cleaned up her face. "Sorry, Peter," she said. "I'm not often seasick. But this has been a rather upsetting day."

Simon was methodically lashing Potterton's ankles with one of *Princess Charming*'s sail tyers. Since he was also handcuffed, with George sitting over him, he seemed safe enough for the moment, and I asked Simon to go back to *Lisa* and get our whisky bottle. I hauled in *Lisa* while he handed me the bottle and some cups. Then I poured a drink for Anthea.

She pushed it away but with a little smile that showed that she was coming back to life. "No, Peter, not again!" she said.

"Well I need a drink, anyway," I said. "What about you George? And Simon? I reckon we all need one."

Simon was back in *Princess Charming*. Neither he nor George needed any pressing, and I poured out three stiff drinks. Potterton was making noises. "What about me?" he said.

"What about you?" George said roughly.

"I suppose we're going to do a deal, so you might as well give me a drink. I'm damned uncomfortable like this," Potterton said.

"You can go to hell," said George.

"What do you mean? How much do you want?" Potterton said in a rather puzzled way.

George was speechless.

"I think you are under some misapprehension," I said to Potterton. "You are talking to Chief Superintendent George Payne of the CID."

"What difference does that make? What policeman would say No to £50,000?"

Simon went forward, lifted Potterton's head, and slapped him hard, coldly and deliberately on each cheek. "Sorry," he said to George. "I know policemen mustn't hit people, but I'm not a policeman. I just couldn't stand that."

George held out his hand with real warmth. "I don't think I'm going to arrest you this time," he said to Simon. "But I must arrest this—er—man." To Potterton he said, "Angus Potterton, you are under arrest, for attempted murder and on other charges that will be specified later. You will be given an opportunity to make a statement when we get ashore, but I must warn you that anything you say from now on may be used in evidence."

Potterton spat, futilely, on to the floorboards of his yawl.

George said to Simon, "Keep an eye, and if necessary, a hand, on him. I'm going back to our own boat to call up the Navy."

I hauled in *Lisa* for him. He went on board and began fiddling with one of the walkie-talkie sets. To my astonishment, it worked. "I've got the frigate *Oxford*, Lieut. Commander Saunders. He wants to know where we are? Where exactly are we, Peter?"

I wasn't at all sure. Potterton had picked up the buoyed package from the tanker some distance west of the rendezvous point, but how far west I had no means of knowing. In the strong easterly, we were making a good deal of leeway, again westwards. Visibility was now so poor that I could barely make out the coast five or six miles away. I did some rapid dead reckoning in my head, and called back to George. "Tell him that we're somewhere between Bolt Head and Bolt Tail, about five miles offshore," I said. "I can't be more precise because I can't see anything to take a bearing on."

George had a conversation with the frigate. Then he signed off, and came back to *Princess Charming*. "They're coming to look for us," he said. "They're on station, about ten miles west of the rendezvous."

"We may have drifted a couple of miles more or less towards them," I said, "which means that they may not have much more than eight miles to come. But I don't like it, George. The wind's rising every minute—and just look at that sea!"

A towering, grey mass of water was bearing down on us. Mercifully the two yawls rose to it and it passed under us without breaking, but we were thrown down into the hollow after it with a sickening lurch.

"We can't stay together like this," I said. "We've got to get under way." A horrible thought had struck me after our last lurch, and I called urgently to Simon, "Go forward and make that bloody package fast—we've gone to enough trouble to get it. Use the painter." Then I turned to George. "You're the boss," I said, "but I feel responsible for the marine party. We're all right for the moment, but we may not be all right for many minutes longer. The weather's turning hellish. In this wind, even with the engines, it would be a brutal slog to try to beat back to Salcombe. Our best bet is to run for Plymouth. It can't be more than fourteen or fifteen miles— say four hours' sailing. With any luck the frigate will spot us and escort us in—it would be no joke trying to take us on board in this sea. But we can't count on being spotted. So what I suggest is this. It's too much of a risk to leave Potterton and the evidence of heroin-smuggling in one boat. Let's put Potterton in *Lisa*, and Simon and I will sail her in. You stay here with Anthea and the evidence. Anthea's more or less recovered now, and she's quite capable of handling the yawl with you to help her. We'll try to keep in sight, but it's not easy, and if we do lose sight of each other, don't worry. These yawls are fine boats in a rough sea. We can't miss Plymouth—and as soon as it begins to get dark, we'll pick up the Eddystone Light. And if anything did go wrong with one of us—well, the other would still have a lot of evidence."

It was a hard decision for George, but he could not have got where he was without being able to take decisions. He considered for about fifteen seconds—then we were all but rolled over by another sea. "Okay, Peter," he said. "And good luck."

We waited for a momentarily calm patch to bring *Lisa* alongside. George and Simon heaved Potterton into her without ceremony. I held Anthea's hand for a second and whispered, "God bless you, Sir Anthea." She said nothing, but squeezed my hand hard.

Simon and I followed Potterton into *Lisa*. George gave me Potterton's pistol. "I shouldn't think he *can* give us any trouble now," he said, "but if by any chance he works loose or anything, don't hesitate to use this." I asked for the key to Potterton's handcuffs—not that I had any thought of freeing him, but if we had a capsize or got driven ashore we should have, I supposed, to give him a chance of life. I put the pistol and the key in my pocket, and gave George two of the three walkie-talkie sets. Then I pushed *Lisa* clear of *Princess Charming* with the boathook, and cast off. Anthea freed *Princess Charming*'s backed jib, and at once she began to gather way. "Put another reef in the main when you get it up," I called to them.

Lisa was steadied by her mizzen, and before getting more sail on her we manoeuvred Potterton into a sitting position forward of the centre-plate, with his back against the mast. His hands were still handcuffed behind his waist and his ankles tied together. Simon put a lashing round his body and made this fast to the foot of the mast, so that if we heeled suddenly he could not go overboard. Then we raised the jib and the mainsail, putting in three reefs.

As soon as we were properly under way I asked Simon to take the tiller, and had a go at the walkie-talkie set.

"Yawl *Lisa* calling HMS *Oxford*. Yawl *Lisa* calling HMS *Oxford*. Over," I said.

I got a reply almost at once. "*Oxford* to yawl *Lisa*. Receiving you loud and clear. Proceed. Over."

"Yawl *Lisa* to *Oxford*," I called back. "Position about five miles south west of Ham Stone between Bolt Head and Bolt Tail. Two yawls proceeding Plymouth under sail, course approximately 312 degrees True. Yawl *Princess Charming*, Chief Superintendent George Payne, has contraband. Yawl *Lisa*, Major Peter Blair, has prisoner. All well, but conditions rough. Over."

"*Oxford* to *Lisa*," they came back. "Message received and understood. Will try to intercept you. Have you a radar reflector? If so, please hoist. Over."

Fog in the Channel is such a likely hazard that I did carry a radar reflector on *Lisa*, but I hadn't thought to hoist it. Obviously it would be a help to the frigate to pick us up on her radar screen. I got the reflector from the locker and sent it up to the spreader arm. Then I called the frigate again to tell them I had done so. "*Oxford* to *Lisa*. Thank you very much," they replied.

We were moving fast, but in somewhat dicey conditions with the wind, now a near-gale, almost astern of us, with the constant risk of an involuntary gybe. I wondered whether to take the mainsail off her, but she went better with the reefed sail, so I left it up. But I took in her working jib and substituted the small storm jib. Anthea had done the same. *Princess Charming* was about a quarter of a mile inshore of us, going well.

Potterton was in a bad way. It was bitterly cold, and trussed up as he was he couldn't move much. Warning Simon to watch out for a gybe, I left him at the tiller and got out a couple of blankets, which I wrapped round Potterton, covering the lot with a spare oilskin coat. Then I got one of our remaining flasks and got a cup of hot, sweet coffee down him—at least I got most of it down him, for with his hands tied he couldn't hold the cup himself, and in holding it to his lips a fair bit got spilled as *Lisa* jumped about. Feeding him was an odd sensation. I disliked touching him, and had to force myself to do it.

The hot drink and the warmth of the blankets revived him somewhat.

"So you did steal Gwen's locket," he said. "I thought that you were out for yourself—it never occurred to me that you'd be mixed up with the police. But you're a fool, you know. The stuff in that other boat is worth anything up to half a million pounds. Why not share it?"

Simon called out urgently, "Peter, I think you'd better take her. It's horribly tricky steering."

I went aft and relieved him at the helm. The yawl was certainly a handful. She was sailing fast, and it would have been a grand, exhilarating run if the sea had been less broken. As it was, she would make a breathtaking leap from a crest to be stopped or slewed-round by a cross sea. You had to watch for these cross seas, and fight with the tiller to keep her going with the wind on the weather side of the mainsail to prevent a gybe. Again I considered dropping the main, and again I decided against it. She could still stand the reefed main, and it was contributing a lot of drive. It would have been more comfortable to alter course and bring the wind abeam by standing out to sea, but that would mean hours longer before we could hope to reach Plymouth. I was worried about Potterton, and felt that the sooner he could be locked up under cover, the better. We had to keep going as we were.

I could still see *Princess Charming* through the gathering murk. Anthea had brought her a little nearer to us, and it was comforting to see how well she handled her. Poor girl, I thought. She would have a long spell at the helm. George was all right as a good muscular foredeckhand, but he had little experience at sea and could not be left at the tiller in conditions like these.

Simon had gone forward to keep an eye on Potterton. "Better rub his arms and legs a bit," I said.

He didn't relish the job, but set about it dutifully.

Potterton said, "Can you undo my hands so that I can do this for myself?"

"No," I replied.

"What a bastard you are," he said.

Simon stopped his massage. "You'd better be careful, Potterton," he warned. "I've hit you once, and I'd enjoy hitting you again."

Potterton was quiet for a bit. Then he said, "There's no need to treat me like this. Can you at least wipe my glasses?

I can't see a thing, and the spray's dripping off them and freezing on my face."

Simon removed the glasses, and then he called to me, "Peter, have you anything to wipe them with? My handkerchief's under three layers of oilies and pullovers."

"Give them to me," I said. He handed me the glasses, and with my arm hooked round the tiller I got out my own handkerchief to clean them. As I wiped the lenses I suppose I looked through them, and suddenly I noticed something odd. They were plain glass!

My mind went back to the inquest on Edna Brown. I saw Potterton stand up to offer to pay for Edna Brown's funeral, and I remembered how he had taken off his glasses for a moment to polish them. I remembered Miss Wilberforce, and her solicitors' office, and her remark about feeling that she had seen Potterton somewhere before. I had a sudden, blinding sense of certainty. I handed back the glasses to Simon, who put them on Potterton's face. And I said:

"Your name is not Angus Potterton. You are Rupert Hare."

For the second time the man we called Potterton spat; luckily for him he did not spit at Simon, but against the wind at me. Then he laughed. "What the hell difference does it make?" he said.

"It may give you a bit longer in prison."

"You can't get longer than life. And I don't think I'll stay in prison very long—I've got a lot of friends, you know, Blair. So all right, I'll tell you. Yes, I am Rupert Hare."

"Why didn't you stay in South America?"

"Didn't care for it much. And I didn't have any money. I met a man who had business interests in—er—importing, and came back to run this end of the business. I couldn't exactly come back as Rupert Hare."

"You didn't have any money? What about all those Swiss bank accounts?"

He laughed again. "Newspaper talk, Blair. I did have a lot of money, yes, but it was all tied up in that big property deal in the Midlands. If that fool of a Town Clerk hadn't lost his nerve and killed himself I'd have made a lot more. So, incidentally, would he—a point you might think about now, Blair. But that bastard let me down, and when the balloon went up I was stretched to the limit. When I thought it was tactful to go to South America I bought an air ticket on one of my credit cards. Do you know, I don't think that account has ever been paid? How careless one gets!"

"I still don't understand. What happened to Angus Potterton? There is a real Angus Potterton."

"Angus and I were at school together. Apart from the fact that he wore glasses and I didn't we were very much alike—ridiculously alike, considering that we weren't related at all. Angus was always out to make a bit, and sometimes I'd pay him to stand in for me if I wanted to cut school. If he took off his glasses he could pass for me, anywhere. He was a dull stick, but he could be useful, and when I was in the property market he did a fair bit of Public Relations work for me. When I had to come back from South America I naturally thought of old Angus to help me out. He did."

"What happened to him? Where is he?"

"He went for a sea voyage, like Gwen. Only unlike her, blast her, he didn't come back."

An extraordinary change had come over the man. It was as if his identification as Rupert Hare had enabled him to shed one personality, which he didn't much like, and put on a new—or old—one, which he did. Whatever it was, it was horrible. He was triumphant now, boastful, glorying in his own cleverness.

"Why did you kill Gwen?" I asked.

"Because she was a silly little bitch. She was doing very well for herself when she went and fell in love, or thought she'd fallen in love, with some damned student she'd met.

She said she was going to have a child by him. I told her not to be a fool, and I actually arranged for her to get rid of the child, when she turned nasty and began talking a lot of nonsense about wanting to live her own life. So she had to go. Don't you think she made her exit rather well? That note of hers, well, almost hers, it really brought tears to my eyes when I wrote it. But she let me down, you know, with that damned locket. I made things easy for her because, after all, she'd done a lot for me in the past. Just a knock on the head, then I gave her a hefty fix. She'd always kept clear of the stuff herself, so it acted pretty quickly. Then a nice sea voyage. She had to be alive you see, so that she could drown, but I fixed it so she wouldn't know anything about it. But I forgot her bloody locket. I saw it as soon as she went in and I tried to get it back with the boathook, but I was hitting her face so much with the hook that I must have pushed her down. Anyway, she just sank and the bloody locket with her. It ought to have been all right..."

I suppose I was too intent on listening to notice the big cross-sea ahead of us. *Lisa* gave a sickening lurch, and I couldn't correct it in time. The wind got behind the mainsail and sent it crashing over in a gybe. It hit the shroud with savage force, and the sail split to ribbons. I thought that the shroud and mast would surely go. *Lisa* broached to, and went over on her beam ends. A mass of water came on board.

Somehow, the shroud and mast didn't go. I leaped for the halliard to get the dangerous boom and screaming rags of sail under control. Miraculously, for the weight of water in her, *Lisa* righted herself. Then I looked to see what had happened to Potterton. But the man we called Potterton was gone. The lashing that had held him to the mast was cleanly cut. Simon was just putting away his sheath knife.

"We must get some of this water out of her," I said. "Simon, you use the bucket. I'll work the bilge pump."

Lisa was more or less lying a-hull, but she floated, and by baling and pumping between us we gradually got enough water out of her to make her seaworthy again. Anthea had seen our knockdown, and came over as close as she dared, but there was nothing she or George could do. They stood by us until it was clear that we were not going to sink. The wind made it next to impossible to get any words across, and I had no loud hailer. But I managed to convey that we were all right, and that Potterton was gone. Anthea sensibly went a little upwind of us so that George could shout to us. "Look after yourselves," he said. "And we've still got the heroin." They got under way, and were soon out of sight ahead of us.

With that wind astern of us we could make fair progress with a headsail and the mizzen. I thought of putting back the working jib, but decided against it. The engine was for the moment waterlogged and useless, but if we didn't get knocked down again, we might be able to start it later. It was comforting to be jogging on our way again. It was futile to think of looking for Hare (or Potterton). Handcuffed, and with his feet tied, he must have gone down like a stone.

Simon helped me to tidy up. Then he said in a matter of fact way, "That was my child he was speaking of, although he called her Gwen. What do you suppose I'll get for cutting him loose?"

"In a sane world, a medal, I should think," I said. "With the world as it is, the remains of that lashing had better go overboard. We don't want anybody noticing those cut ends."

The lashing duly followed Potterton. I threw it overboard myself.

I thought I'd better report things to the Navy. The walkie-talkie was in a waterproof jacket, and still worked. "Yawl *Lisa* to *Oxford*. I have a message for you. Over," I said.

"*Oxford* to *Lisa*. Proceed. Over."

"*Lisa* to *Oxford*. Regret we have suffered a knockdown.

Prisoner lost overboard. Mainsail also lost. Proceeding Plymouth under reduced rig. Yawl *Princess Charming* safe. Making for Plymouth ahead of us under reefed mainsail, mizzen and storm jib. Over."

"*Oxford* to *Lisa*. Sorry about mishap," they called back. "We have you on our radar screen, and you should see us in about twenty minutes. Over and out."

It was getting dark, and it was actually about half an hour later when we picked up the frigate's lights. I sent up a white flare, and a few minutes afterwards the frigate had us in her searchlight. We could talk only by radio. I said that we were all right, and that it was too rough to attempt to come on board. They agreed, but said that they would stand by us to accompany us to Plymouth. We made it about three hours later. Anthea and George had beaten us by a good hour.

12

The Last of the Locket

THE IDENTIFICATION OF the man we had called Potterton with Rupert Hare explained a lot of things. George was less disturbed about his disappearance than I had feared. He was quite philosophical. "It's a pity we couldn't bring him to trial," he said, "but what would have happened? We'd have convicted him of Gwen Rosing's murder, but I doubt if we'd even have charged him with murdering Potterton. We'd have got him for attempted murder by shooting at us from his boat, and he would have been convicted on the heroin charge, and on various charges still on the file from the Whitehall scandals. He would have got life on the murder charge, and long sentences on the others—maybe the judge would have recommended that he should serve at least twenty years, or maybe thirty years. What of it? Can you reform a man like him? Two murders that we know of, perhaps others that we don't. Three suicides brought about by his greed, several lives wrecked by his corruption in the Whitehall case, more destroyed by his heroin pushing. For most of my life I've been against capital punishment, and I was glad when it was abolished. Now I'm not so sure. You don't need to be a policeman to know that there's evil in the world, but as a policeman it's brought home to you in a way that some people don't understand. And what do you do about evil except try to root it out? Of course there are plenty of criminals—even bad criminals—who have a lot of good in them, who *can* be reformed, and helped into being decent citizens. Hare wasn't like that. Consistently, all his life, he was a corrupter of others. He'd have gone on trying to corrupt people in prison—don't forget, you can corrupt people in prison. The only sane sentence for him other than death would have been solitary confinement for life, and that's so horrible to contemplate that no civilised society could tolerate it. Death? Yes. I know the arguments, and I accept most of them, but yet there are some people so steeped in evil, so capable of harming others, that I don't know. Thank God I don't have to judge. I shan't lose any sleep over what happened to Hare, and I hope you won't, Peter."

"No," I said. "I don't think I shall lose any sleep."

Although they could not bring Hare to trial, the police made a tremendous haul. While we were in the Channel, Commander Seddon and a detachment from his drug squad raided the premises of Knowledge Exchange, and got enough evidence to smash that vile organisation and to send six men and two women to prison. Perhaps even more important in the long run, a major international organisation for smuggling heroin was smashed. The submarine in the Channel shadowed the tanker *Mount Vernon* to Rotterdam, where she was met by a highly expert party of Dutch police and Customs Officers. Her crew from the master downwards were arrested. Three of them, who had not been happy about what was being done, broke down under questioning, and the whole story came out. The *Mount Vernon* belonged to a shipping firm which specialised in short term charters, providing tankers for individual voyages, to make good gaps in the oil companies' regular fleets, when one of their own ships was damaged, or delayed for some reason. That meant that she was liable to be sent all over the world, although she was almost bound to make three or four trips a year from the Middle East to Western Europe. An oil company executive in the Middle East, who had developed a profitable sideline in drug smuggling, persuaded her master to deliver small quantities of heroin whenever she called in his area. The fact that she had no fixed run was a great help, because supplies could be smuggled through many different ports, but the necessity to smuggle the heroin ashore in personal belongings or clothing meant that only small quantities could be delivered.

The oilman concerned had been transferred to South America, where Hare met him. Hare's property-empire having collapsed, he was (as he had told us) very short of money. He was plausible enough to swindle a few tourists, but he didn't know Spanish and he wanted to get his hands on big money again. He was in fact trying to interest the oil executive in a wholly fraudulent scheme for smuggling cocaine into the United States—he had no access to supplies of cocaine, and there would never have been any—when it turned out that drug smuggling was a subject that the oil man really did know something about. Hare then thought up the dinghy smuggling scheme for getting heroin into England. This so impressed the oil executive that he decided to go back to the Middle East and make drug smuggling his main business, and he financed Hare's return to England. He got hold of the papers of a seaman on an oil tanker who had died, and got Hare a job in the dead man's name in the crew of another tanker. That was how Hare managed to get back to England without attracting attention.

In England, he had his private plan for getting rid of Angus Potterton and taking his identity, which he proceeded to do. He was quite capable of running Potterton's business, and tactfully went into a nursing home for a couple of months, during which he got rid of the real Potterton's secretary by giving her a year's wages and explaining that illness made it necessary for him to reconstruct the firm. Safely inaccessible in the nursing home, he got rid similarly of the two or three executives or "associates" who had been with

Potterton for any length of time. He then recovered, made new appointments from the fluid world of Public Relations, and brought in Gwen Rosing to keep an eye on the staff and help him generally. Then he established Knowledge Exchange, at first as an entirely innocent book distributing business, but really to be his agency for drug distribution.

While Hare was establishing himself as Potterton in London, his partner was arranging things in the Middle East. Dinghy smuggling made it possible to send consignments of heroin a hundredweight or so at a time. The profits were enormous. The whole crew of the *Mount Vernon* had to be paid to keep quiet, and the bonus given to each man was about four times his normal annual wage. The police spent months in trying to unravel Potterton-Hare's various bank accounts and investments. They were by no means certain that they had uncovered all of them, but what they did unearth suggested that he had been making at least £300,000 a year. The ex-oil executive, who was an American, was arrested in Hong Kong, where he owned a number of businesses under a variety of names. A complicated legal process then started, to determine where he should be tried. It was beginning to look as if he would have to face the stern anti-drug laws of Iran, where conviction carries a death penalty, when he saved everybody trouble by committing suicide with an overdose of presumably his own heroin, which he contrived to have smuggled to him in the remand prison.

The partnership's chief difficulty was in the *Mount Vernon*'s irregular routes—what had been an advantage in smuggling heroin in small quantities was a major disadvantage when it came to shipping it by the hundredweight. No one in the shipping company was implicated, but various employees in shipbrokers' offices were recruited to keep an eye on her movements. The code messages were necessary because she might be diverted to the Channel at short notice: her master always kept a consignment or two of heroin hidden away on board, so a buoyed package could be thrown overboard whenever there was a dinghy waiting to receive it. When he knew that he had a destination that would take him up-Channel, he would work out a date and rendezvous position, and send a coded message to the partnership's shipping agent in the nearest convenient country. The agent would then arrange for it to be published in the personal column of *The Examiner*. The *Mount Vernon* had made several voyages to French ports, which explained the Paris origin of some of the messages. The last message, from Rome, was brought about by a sudden change of plan. The *Mount Vernon* was on her way out light to the Persian Gulf when she was diverted to Libya to pick up a cargo of oil for Rotterdam. In Libya, her master had sent his message to the partnership's agent in Italy, who had used a Rome advertising agency to send it to *The Examiner*.

All this did not come to light at once, but was pieced together by police questioning of individuals in several different countries, and from the evidence that was given at various trials. For some weeks we wondered if Hare's body would be brought ashore as Gwen Rosing's was, but he did not return from his own sea voyage. The raid on Knowledge Exchange made a big story for the newspapers, and a police statement that the man calling himself Angus Potterton had been identified as Rupert Hare made it bigger still. But Hare was dead, and the authorities decided that Edna Brown should remain buried as Edna Brown. So Gwen Rosing passed out of history, having more than made up in death for whatever sins she committed in her short, unhappy life.

George had to face a barrage of interviewers, but he did it very well, and was discreetly vague about the various parts played by Simon, Anthea, and me. Shortly afterwards he was made chief constable of a neighbouring West Country police force. Seddon also got a well deserved promotion, and so did Sergeant Manning. Pusey got a knighthood in the next Birthday Honours, but the outside world was left to assume that this was a normal step upwards in the Home Office hierarchy; his part in the unravelling of the Hare-Potterton case was not mentioned. He invited George, Anthea and me to a private dinner party in his flat to celebrate his knighthood. I showed him a letter I had just had from Simon, in Alaska. He wrote,

"... somehow I can never think of Sheila as having been in any way the same person as Edna Brown and Gwen Rosing. It seems to me that my Sheila was real, and they were—I don't know. Perhaps actresses playing parts that life forced them into..."

"Have you still got the locket?" I asked.
"Yes," said Sir Edmund. "It's in my safe at the Home Office."
"Do you think we could send it to Simon—without the contents of course?"
"It would be highly irregular," said Sir Edmund, "but why not? If anything belonged to a real woman, that did."

تمام شود